W9-CWT-667

Sojourner's Truth
& other stories

Lee Maracle

Sojourner's Truth
& other stories

PRESS GANG PUBLISHERS

VANCOUVER

Canadian Cataloguing in Publication Data

Maracle, Lee, 1950-
   Sojourner's Truth

   ISBN 0-88974-023-2

   I. Title.
PS8576.A72S6   1990   C813'.54   C90-091571-4
PR9199.3.M37S6   1990

The story *Worm* was originally published in *Frictions*, edited by Rhea Tregebov (Toronto: Second Story Press, 1989)

First Printing December 1990
   1   2   3   4   5   95   94   93   92   91   90

The Publisher acknowledges financial assistance from the Canada Council.

Consulting Editor: Beth Brant
Editor for the Press: Barbara Kuhne
Design and production by Val Speidel
© Cover image from a black and white photograph by Glenda J. Guilmet, "Shadow Dance #9," 1989
© Author photograph by Brenda Hemsing, 1990
Typeset in 11/13 Goudy Oldstyle; Linotronic output at The Typeworks
Printed on acid free paper
Printed by Hignell Printing Ltd.
Printed and bound in Canada

Press Gang Publishers
603 Powell Street
Vancouver, B.C. V6A 1H2 Canada

*Dedicated to all those Native people who find themselves
staring at a blank white sheet and struggle to talk to it...*

Other Books by Lee Maracle

I Am Woman (Write-on Press, North Vancouver)
Bobbi Lee: Indian Rebel (Women's Press, Toronto)
Seeds (poetry), (Write-on Press, North Vancouer)
Telling It: Women and Language Across Cultures, co-editor
(Press Gang Publishers, Vancouver)
Linked Lives (Renga poetry), co-author, edited by Ayanna Black and
Doré Michelut (Editions Trois, Montreal)

Acknowledgements

I want to thank all those Native people I have met, living or dead, who helped me to find my voice and provided me with an endless run of stories and a deep sense of loyalty to ourselves. I would like to thank Beth Brant who struggled to get the best possible words from me. Barbara Kuhne and Press Gang Publishers for nagging my book into being. Dennis Maracle for relieving me of the tension of copy editing and coming to grips with the bureaucracy necessary to complete a book. I wish to acknowledge my mother for giving me Maggie and letting me read and scribble when I should have been helping her. Thanks to Eunice Brooks for being herself, untainted by the world's attitudes and last, but not least, I want to thank my children for becoming the wonderful young adults you are, despite having a writer who has had precious little time for you, instead of a devoted mother.

Contents

Preface

You Become the Trickster

In the course of writing these stories I tried very hard to integrate two mediums: oratory and European story, our sense of metaphor, our use of it, with traditional European metaphor and story form. I also sought out stories from my life, my imagination and my history that contained an element of the universal. Always I clung to the principles of oratory. Each story is layered with unresolved human dilemmas; each story will require the engaged imagination of the reader.

Short story in European form has a beginning, a middle and an end; a plot line, a climax and a conclusion, all of which are held together by a single metaphor which weaves itself through the fabric of the story. It is entertaining and possesses an inherent truth which is transformative both for the reader and the characters within the story. Had I continued school long enough and taken enough European creative writing courses I would know what all the metaphors are and would be able to match metaphor to subject. I didn't, not because I doubted I could grasp the elements of story and turn them to my account, but because I would have lost myself in the transliteration of our story to European story.

Our story-telling is much different from the European story. Like in a European story there is a plot—that is, something happens, events occur, the characters are caught in a dilemma—and there is a conclusion. The difference is that the reader is as much a part of the story as the teller. Most of our stories don't have orthodox "conclusions"; that is left to the listeners, who we trust will draw useful lessons from the story—not necessarily the lessons we wish them to draw, but all conclusions are considered valid. The listeners are drawn into the dilemma and are expected at some point in their lives to actively work themselves out of it.

The word story-teller is inappropriate here: *to tell, to explain.* When our orators get up to tell a story, there is no explanation, no set-up to guide the listener—just the poetic terseness of the dilemma is presented. There is only one such story in this collection. I have tried on a half dozen occasions to "rewrite" it, to no avail. With some dilemmas the drama of it, the poetry of it, is best left intact. For me, the drama, the very dilemma, is spoiled by framing it in orthodox European story style.

This is most disturbing for European readers/listeners. Much of their condition of life hinges on instructive learning. We have not been battered with such learning techniques as "don't touch this and don't do that." Our character is carefully cultivated by stories told at night that are amusing and, for us, instructive. Though we as children must fill in the conclusion, we don't seem to have a great deal of difficulty doing that. Consequently, we grow bored quickly under European instruction. We firmly believe as eight-year-olds that school is stupid, repetitive and lacking in dignity. We begin to daydream—like "Charlie," in the story with that title—after the first five minutes of instruction. Not much is left to the imagination in European stories either. The answer to the question posed lies within the lines of the story. The reader must figure out from the use of metaphor, the events and the character what the point of transformation or the value of the story is. Our stories merely pose the dilemma.

In these stories I've had to delete some wonderful moments in the listening process. When our orators get up to speak, they move in metaphorical ways. Anyone who has watched our speakers is familiar with the various faces of the orator. Each facial expression, change in tone of voice, cadence or diction has meaning for us. I have watched such orators as Philip Paul, George Manuel and Ellen White pull the legs of government officials by posturing raven while complimenting the official. For us this is hilarious, because not only does the posture go over the heads of the official listening, but also because the joke does not go by the Native audience watching the interplay. The silent language of physical metaphor is a story in itself. I substitute physical description for physical metaphor.

In the writing of these stories I tried very hard to draw the reader into the centre of the story, in just the same way the listener of our oral stories is drawn in. At the same time the reader must remain central to the working out of the drama of life presented. As listener/reader, you become the trickster, the architect of great social transformation at whatever level you choose.

Bertha

The accumulation of four days of rain reflected against the street lamps and the eternal night-time neon signs, bathing the pavement in a rainbow of crystal splashes. In places on the road it pooled itself into thin sheets of blue-black glass from which little rivulets slipped away, gutter bound. From eaves and awnings the rain fell in a steady flow; even the signposts and telephone poles chattered out the sounds of the rain before the drops split themselves on the concrete sidewalks. Everywhere the city resounded with the heavy rhythm of pelting rain. It cut through the distorted bulk of the staggering woman.

The woman did not notice the rain. Instead, the bulk that was Bertha summoned all her strength, repeatedly trying to correctly determine the distance between herself and the undulating terra beneath her feet to prevent falling. Too late. She fell again. She crawled the rest of the way to the row of shacks. Cannery row, where the very fortunate employees of the very harassed and worried businessmen reside, is not what one might call imaginatively designed. The row consists of one hundred shacks, identical in structure, sitting attached by common walls in a single row. The row begins on dry land and ends over the inlet. Each shack is one storey high and about eighteen by twenty feet in floor space.

They are not insulated. The company had more important sources of squander for its profits: new machines had to be bought, larger executive salaries had to be paid—all of which severely limited the company's ability to extend luxuries to the producers of its canned fish. The unadorned planks which make up the common walls at the back and front of each shack and at the end of each row are all that separate people from nature. A gable roof begins about seven feet from the floor and comes to a peak some eight feet later. Each roof by this time enjoyed the same number of unrepaired holes as its neighbour, enabling even the gentlest of drizzles in. The holes, not being part of the company's construction plan, are more a fringe benefit or a curse of natural unrepaired wear, depending on your humour.

None of the buildings are situated on the ground. All were built of only the sturdiest wood and were well creosoted at the base to fend off rot for at least two decades. Immersed in salt water and raw sewage as they have been this past half century, they are beginning to show a little wear. In fact, once during the usual Saturday night rough-housing which takes place on a pay night, X pitched his brother over the side. They had been arguing about whether the foreman was a pig or a dog. X maintained dogs did not stink and what is more, could be put to work, while his brother held he would not eat a dog, and food being a much higher use-value, the foreman was a dog. He then let go with a string of curses at X, which brought X to grievous violence. On the way to the salt chuck X's brother knocked out one of the pilings. It was never replaced. The hut remains precariously perched on three stilts and is none the worse for that. Unfortunately, the water that filled X's brother's lungs settled the argument forever. The accused foreman has since been known as a pig.

Not to discredit the company. In the days before modern machinery, when the company had to employ a larger number of workers to process less fish, it used cheaper paint—whitewash to be honest. One day all the workers who had congregated in the town at the season's opening beheld a fine sight at the end of Main Street: exterior house paint of the most durable quality. These stains come in a variety of colours but the company, not wishing to spoil its workers with excessive finery, stuck with the colour which by then had achieved historical value.

The paint did not really impress anyone save the foreman. So delighted was he with the new paint that he mentioned it time and again, casually. The best response he got was one low grunt from one of the older, more polite workers. Most simply stared at their superior with a profoundly empty look. *Thankless ingrates,* he told himself, though he dared not utter any such thing aloud.

Although the opinion of the foreman about his workers had stood the test of time over the decade that had lapsed, the paint job had not been so lucky. The weather had been cruel to the virgin stain, ripping the white in ugly gashes from the row's simple walls. The rigorous climate of the North West Coast destroyed the paint in a most consistent way, exactly with the run of the wood grain. Where the grain grooved, the stain remained; where the grain ridged, the salt sea wind and icy rain tore the stain off.

At the front of the dwellings some of the doors are missing. Not a lot of them, mind you, certainly not the majority have gone astray. The plank boardwalk in front of cannery row completes the picture of the outside. Over the years, at uncannily even intervals, each sixth board has disappeared, some by very bizarre happenstances.

Inside, the huts are furnished with tasteless simplicity. A sturdy, four-legged cedar table of no design occupies the middle of the room. Four wooden, high-backed chairs built with unsteamed two-by-twos and a square piece of good-one-side plywood surround the table. The floors are shiplap planks. Squatted in the centre of the back wall is a pot-bellied cast-iron stove, though those workers who still cook use a Coleman. Shelving above the pot-bellied stove keeps the kitchenware and food supplies immodestly in view. Two bunks to the right and two to the left complete the furnishings. It was not the sort of place in which any of the workers felt inspired to add a touch of their personal self. No photos, no knick-knacks. What the company did not provide, the workers did not have.

The residence, taken as a whole, was not so bad but for

one occasional nuisance. At high-tide each dwelling, except the few nearest shore, was partially submerged in water. It wasn't really such a great bother. After all, the workers spent most of their waking time at the cannery—upwards of ten hours a day, sometimes this included Sunday, but not always—and the bunks were sufficiently far from the floor such that sleeping, etc., carried on unencumbered. A good pair of Kingcome slippers* was all that was needed to prevent any discomfort the tide caused. The women who used to complain violently to the company that their cooking was made impossible by such intrusions have long since stopped. After the strike of '53 cooking was rendered redundant as the higher wage afforded the women restaurant fare at the local town's greasy spoon. Besides which, the sort of tides that crept into the residence occurred but twice or thrice a season. Indeed, the nuisance created was trifling.

Bertha is on the "sidewalk" crawling. The trek across Main Street to the boardwalk had taken everything out of Bertha.

"F.ck.ng btstsh" dribbles from her numb lips.

She glances furtively from side to side. The indignity of her position does not escape her. Being older than most of her co-workers, she is much more vulnerable to the elements. Bertha donned all the sweaters she brought to cannery row and her coat to keep warm. She spent the whole night drinking in the rain on the hill behind the city and now all of her winter gear is water-logged. The fifteen extra pounds make it impossible for her to move. She curses and prays no one sees her.

Her short pudgy fingers clutch at the side of residence No. 13 in an effort to rise above her circumstances. She is gaining the upper hand when a mocking giggle slaps her about the head and ears.

---

*hip waders

"F.ck.ng btstsh"

Trapped. Emiserated. Resigned. What the hell? She is no different from anyone else. Her memory reproaches her with the treasure of a different childhood. A childhood filled with the richness of every season, when not a snowflake fell unnoticed. Her memory retreats to another time.

* * *

The early autumn sunlight danced across lush green hillsides. Diamond dew drops glistened from each leaf. Crisp air and still warm sun excited the youth. Chatter and bantering laughter filled the air. Bertha in her glory punched out one-liners and smiled at the approval of the old ladies who chuckled behind their aging hands. Things were different then. Each girl was born in the comfort of knowing how she would grow, bear children and age with dignity to become a respected matriarch.

On the hills, basket on her back, Bertha was not called Bertha. She wanted to hear her name again, but something inside her fought against its articulation. In her new state of shame she could not whisper, even to herself, the name she had taken as woman. Old Melly staggered into view, eyes twinkling. Bertha didn't really want to see her now.

"Hey Bertie," the giggle hollered out her nickname, unmindful of the woman's age and her own youth. "I got some wine."

"Khyeh, hyeh, yeh" and the circle of memory that crept out at her from the fog dimmed, but refused to recede. You had another upbringing before all this, the memory chided her. The efforts of the village women to nurture her as keeper of her clan, mother of all youth, had gone to naught. Tears swole from behind her eyes. "Damn wine," she muttered to herself. In the autumn hills of her youth the dream of motherhood had already begun to fade. Motherhood, the re-creation of ancient stories that would instruct the young in the laws of her people and encourage good citizenship from even the babies, had eluded her.

In the moment of her self-recrimination, Bertie contemplated going home. Home? Home was a young girl rushing through a meadow, a cedar basket swishing lightly against dew-laden leaves, her nimble fingers plucking ripe fat berries from their branches, the wind playfully teasing and tangling the loose, waist-length black hair that glistened in the autumnal dawn while her mind enjoyed the prospect of becoming... becoming, and the words in English would not come. She remembered the girl, the endless stories told to her, the meanings behind each story, the careful coaching in the truth that lay behind each one, the reasons for their telling, but she could not, after fifty years of speaking crippled English, define where it was all supposed to lead. Now all that remained was the happiness of her childhood memories against the stark emptiness of the years that stretched behind them.

Her education had been cut short when her great-grandfather took a christian name. She remembered a ripple of bewildered tension for which her language had no words to describe or understand what had gone through the village. The stories changed and so did the language. No one explained the intimacies of the new feeling in either language. Confusion, a splitting within her, grew alongside the murmur that beset the village. Uncertainty closed over the children. Now, even the stories she had kept tucked away in her memory escaped her. She stared hard down the narrow boardwalk trying to mark the moment when her memories had changed.

The priest had christened the most important man in the village. Slowly, christians appeared in their ranks. The priest left no stone unturned. Stories, empowering ceremonies, became pagan rituals, pagan rituals full of horrific shame. Even the way in which grooms were chosen changed. The old women lost their counsel seats at the fires of their men. Bighouses were left to die and tiny homes isolated from the great families were constructed. Little houses that separated each sister from the other, harbouring loneliness and isolation. Laughter died within the walls of these little homes. No one connected the stripping of woman-power and its transfer to the priest as the basis for the sudden uselessness all the people felt. Disempowered, the old ladies ceased to tell stories and lived out their lives without taking the children to the hills again.

For a short time, life was easier for everyone. No more shaking cedar, collecting goat hair or carefully raising dogs to spin the wool for their clothing. Trade—cash and the securing of furs by the village men—replaced the work of women. Bertha could not see that the feelings of anxiety among the youth were rooted in the futureless existence that this transfer of power created. A wild and painful need for a brief escape from their new life drove youth to the arms of whiskey traders.

An endless stream of accommodating traders paddled upriver to fleece the hapless converts. Those who lacked trap lines began disappearing each spring to the canneries where cash could be gotten. Young women followed on their heels. The police, too, gained from this new state of affairs. As the number of converts increased so did the number of drinkers. Interdiction caught up with those unfortunates not skilled at dodging the police. Short stays as guests in the queen's hotel* became the basis for a new run of stories, empty of old meaning. The rupture of the old and the rift created was swift and unrelenting. Things could be bought with money, and wages purchased the things of life much more swiftly and in greater quantities than did their pagan practices. Only great-grandmother, much ridiculed for her stubbornness, remained sober and pagan to her death. Her face lingered in the fog while Bertha wondered why the old woman had stopped talking to her. The process was complete before Bertha was out of

---

*jail

her teens. Then she, too, joined the flow of youth to cannery row.

Bertha had come to cannery row full of plans. Blankets could be purchased with the cash she earned. How could she have known the blankets they sold were riddled with sickness? She paid the trader who delivered the blankets, as had some of the other youth. She experienced the same wild abandon that life outside the watchful eye of grannies and mothers gave rise to. They learned to party away the days of closure when there were not enough fish to work a whole shift. At season's end they all got into their boats and headed home. A lone canoe bobbed in the water just feet from the shore of their village; a solitary old man paddled out to greet them.

"Go back, death haunts the village, go back." Confused, they went back. The story of the blankets did not catch up to them until years later. In their zeal to gift their loved ones they had become their killers. In their confusion and great guilt, wine consoled them.

* * *

Bertha stared blankly at her swollen hands. With blurred vision she peered unsteadily towards hut number nine. It wasn't home. She had no home. Home was fifty years ago and gone. Home was her education forever cut short by christian well-meaning. Home was the impossibility of her ever becoming the intellectual she should have been; it was the silence of not knowing how it all came to pass. Slowly her face found the young girl leaning out of the doorway.

"Ssr."

She lumbered reluctantly to where the giggle sat, her mouth gaping in a wide grin, exposing prematurely rotten teeth. Bertha could hardly look at her. No one as young as this girl should have rotten teeth. It marred her flawlessly even features. The large, thickly-lashed black eyes only sharpened the vileness of bad teeth. What a cruel twist of fate that this girl, whose frame had not yet acquired the bulk that bearing children and rearing them on a steady diet of winter rice and summer wine creates, should be burdened with a toothless grin before her youth was over.

The consumption of wine was still rational in the girl's maiden state, though not for long. Already the regularity of her trips to the bootlegger was beginning to spoil her eyes with occasional shadows. Her delicately shaped face sometimes hinted of a telling puffiness. On days like that it was hard for the girl to pose as a carefree and reckless youth. Today was not such a day.

Bertha hesitated before sitting, staring hard at the jug on the table. Unable to leave, but not quite up to sitting down, she remained rooted to the spot. She struggled with how it came to be that this girl from her village was so foreign to her. The moment threatened the comfort of shallow oblivion the girl needed. A momentary softness came over her face as she beckoned Bertha to sit. "Relax, Bertha, have a drink." Bertha sighed and sat down. The girl shucked the tenderness and resumed her gala self.

By day's end the jug was wasted and so were the women. There had been conversations and moments of silence, sentimental tears had been shed, laughter, even rage and indignation at the liberties white-male-bottom-pinchers took with Native women had been expressed. In all, the drunk had been relatively ordinary, except for a feeling that kept sinking into the room. It seemed to the girl to come from the ceiling and hang over their heads. The feeling was not identifiable and its presence was inexplicable. Nothing in particular brought it on. Only the wine chased the feeling from the windowless room. For the giggle, these moments were sobering, but Bertha seemed unruffled by it. If she was bothered, she betrayed no sign. At such moments, the giggle snatched the bottle and furiously poured the liquid into her throat. The wine instantly returned the young girl's world to its swaying, bleary, much more bearable state.

Bertha rarely left anything started unfinished, even as concerns a jug of wine. But the more she drank the more she realized she did not know this woman, this daughter who was not nurtured by her village grandmothers, but who had left as a small child and never returned to her home. She was so like all the youth who joined the march to cannery row of late. Foreign and mis-educated. Callous? Was that what made them so hard to understand? The brutal realization that she, Bertha, once destined to have been this young woman's teacher, had nothing to give but stories—dim, only half-remembered and barely understood—brought her up short. Guilt drove her from her chair before the bottle was empty. The feeling again sank from the ceiling, shrouding the girl in terror. Foreboding feelings raced through her body, but her addled consciousness could not catch any one of them and hold them long enough for her mind to contemplate their meaning.

Bertha stopped at the door, turned and stumbled back to the shaking girl. She touched her so gently on the cheek that the girl would hardly have been sure it happened except the touch made her eye twitch and the muscles in her face burn. The realization that the gulf between them was too great, their difference entrenched by Bertha's own lack of knowledge, saddened Bertha. Bertha wanted to tell her about her own unspoiled youth, her hills, the berries, the old women, the stories and a host of things she could not find the words for in the English she inherited. It was all so paralyzing and mean. Instead Bertha whispered her sorrow in the gentle words of their ancestors. They were foreign to the girl. The touch, the words, inspired only fear in her. The girl tried to relieve herself by screaming—no sound found its way out of her throat. She couldn't move. The queerly gentle and wistful look on Bertha's face imprinted itself permanently on the memory of the girl. Then Bertha left.

Bertha's departure broke the chains that locked the girl's body to the chair. Her throat broke its silence and a rush of sobs filled her ears. "Damn wine, damn Bertie. Damn," and she grabbed the jug. As the warm liquid jerked to her stomach the feeling floated passively to the ceiling and disappeared. Not convinced that Bertha's departure was final, she flopped the length of her body onto the bunk and prayed for the ill-lit, rat-filled cannery come morning to be upon her soon. Her body grew heavy and her mind dulled. Sleep was near. Before she passed out, her mind caught hold of the notion that she ought to have said goodbye to Bertha. Still, she slept.

*　　*　　*

Bertie's absence at the cannery went unnoticed by all but the foreman. The young girl had blocked the memory of the disturbing evening from her mind. They had been drunk. Probably Bertie's still drunk, ran her reasoning. The foreman, however, being a prudent and loyal company man, thought of nothing else but Bertie's absence. By day's end, he decided by the following reasoning to let her go: Now, one can withstand the not infrequent absences of the younger, swifter and defter of the Native workers. But Bertie is getting old, past her prime, so much so that even her half century of experience compensates little for the disruption of operational smoothness and lost time that her absence gives rise to. Smoothness is essential to any enterprise wishing to realize a profit, and time is money.

This decision was not easily arrived at. He was not totally insensitive to human suffering. He had been kept up all night weighing the blow to Bertie and the reaction of the other workers that firing her might cause, against the company's interest in profits, before finally resolving to fire her. Firing her could produce no results other than her continuing to be a souse. As for the workers, they would be angry but he was sure they wouldn't do anything. In any case, he was the foreman and if he didn't put his foot down these Natives were sure to walk all over him. Her absence again this morning convinced him that he had made the right decision. Still, he could not bring himself to say anything until the end of the day, in case the others decided to walk off the job. No sense screwing up the whole day over one old woman.

In a very loud voice, the foreman informed Bertie's nephew that his auntie Bertie was fired and could he tell her to kindly collect her pay and remove herself by week's end to whence she came.

"Can't be done."

"I beg your pardon and why not? I have every authority to fire every one of you here."

His voice rose and all became quiet but for the hum of machinery. The blood of the workers boiled with shame at the tone of this white man. No one raised their eyes from their fixed position on their work and no one moved.

"Can't be done is all," the nephew flatly replied without looking at the foreman. His hands resumed work, carefully removing the fins from the fish.

"I asked you why not, boy." Angry as he was, he couldn't fire Bertie's nephew. Had he been a shirker, he would have, but Bertie's nephew was one of the more reliable and able of his workers, so he could not fire him. All he could do was sneer "boy" at him and hope that this, the soberest and most regular worker, did not storm out in defiance of the foreman's humiliating remark.

"She's dead."

An agonized scream split the silence and the knife that so deftly beheaded the fish slipped and deprived the lovely young girl of her left thumb and giggle forever.

Who's Political Here?

"Give me that, thanks" and I put the toilet paper back where it belongs, after catching it in mid-air before she managed to throw it into the toilet bowl.

"Excuse me." I grabbed the wash-rag and then both girls, removing them from the temptation of playing in the toilet by pushing them out of the bathroom, while my toothbrush vigorously scraped at my dentures. I strolled into the kitchen. My husband was standing there, looking kind of lost. He had that I'm-about-to-bawl-you-out look, so I started to ignore him before he even spoke.

"Do you think you could do laundry?" he said with the tone of voice that implies it has been at least a month since the last time I had done laundry and in between then and now I had been particularly unproductive. I put my teeth in, ran the water for coffee and mumbled some sort of bored affirmation.

"Could you pass me that hat?" He doesn't. He says something about not having any underwear. I tell him that he certainly does have underwear, that it's in the laundry, and then I crawl over the table, grab the hat, and on jumping to the floor, snatch the matches from one girl's hand, then lean over to turn off the stove the other one has turned on. Thank christ this kitchen is pathetically small. He leaves the room.

"Glgbltglgl-blk-th-blk," my youngest babbles, inflecting her nonsense in a way that suggests she knows what she is trying to say.

"Yeah, I know what you mean, I get that way sometimes too."

"Here, Mommy," the other little girl hands me her sister's shoes. She is three and really does know what's going

on. We are all getting ready to go out. Mothers have an iden-
tifiably different sense of movement when they are getting
ready to go out, and kids know it.

"Stiffen your leg, stiffen your leg... stiffen, that's it,
stiffen... " Oh christ, one of these days she is going to get it,
after all. "*I* stiffen my leg when I put on my shoes." I hold her
on my lap and Tania tries to help. She has reached the age of
insistent and cheerful incompetence. I never discourage her
assistance so everything we do takes twice the time.

"Who are you talking to?" He is back in the room.

"Columpa."

"She can't talk."

"You asked me who I was talking to, not who was talking
to me. What are you going to do today?" I grab the stroller, a
giant second-hand English pram that no longer has the bon-
net or basket, just the frame and seat, and haul it over the
porch to the sidewalk. He has to follow me to answer. I think
this humbling exercise of following me around and answering
my questions annoys him, but he thinks it too petty to men-
tion. Further he is still a little pissed about the underwear
shit—no pun intended. I come back in with him at my heels.

"I'm going to poster downtown." Terrific. He posters
while I maneouver the logistics of shopping, nurturing and
fulfilling my laundress duties. I take the shopping cart and the
two girls and go out again.

"Where are you going? To do the laundry?" If I had the
emotional intensity I would either laugh or cuff him, because
this last remark is so obviously a disguised accusation of my
general recalcitrance, but I have lost the heart to do either.

"Sure."

"How come the cart is empty?"

"I haven't finished shopping," to him, and "Take that
out of your ear," to Columpa. "Only put your elbow in your
ear." She tries, but fails, but keeps trying. At least her mind is
off sticking the pencil in her ear and she doesn't cry when I
put it in my purse.

"You said you were going to do laundry." He is whining now. There is nothing worse than hearing a grown man whine. Grown man. Since when have you known a man to really grow up, Lee. I agree that I am going to do the laundry, today, and put both girls in the stroller (back-to-back), and haul the shopping cart and kids down the lane. He is standing there on the porch looking dejected.

"Hey." I stop without turning around and try to bury the exasperation that wants expression. "You look like one of those sixteenth century fish-mongers, pushing her cart with grim determination." He finds this amusing. One, I don't look like a European anything, and two, the word is fish-wif. Fish-wif means fish-drudge and is the father of wife, but I don't say that. I roll the buggy and pull the cart. I couldn't laugh but I did manage to turn around and give him a condescending smile. He is not an idiot and resents my lack of appreciation for his joke. Another obstacle to hurdle.

"bldthbldbld"

"Cambie wants a cookie," Tania tells me.

"Does she?" Beats me how Tania can understand her babble. Of course, figuring out that the kid wants a cookie can't be too difficult because even if it weren't true, it would at least shut her up and she'd forget what she really did want. Last but not least, Tania's desire for a cookie would be satisfied. I get the cookie, grumbling a whole bunch of stuff about how I never had them as a child, they probably aren't good for you and so forth. They don't care much about all that.

On route to Safeway Columpa addresses every single citizen with a cute little "Hi," four or five times each. Every time she says it Tania insists I look at her and acknowledge her intellectual brilliance—until it about drives me to distraction.

"Hey."

"Sa-aay, Frankie. How are you?" When the only humans you have to talk to are under four and making demands or over thirty and barking out orders, and they all complain when they aren't fulfilled, you really appreciate some guy on the street saying "hey" to you, even if he is an obnoxious womanizer. He sidles over and asks what I am doing. I tell him I am on my way to Safeway to do a little shopping.

"Where are you going to put the groceries?"

"In the cart."

"How the hell are you going to wheel the cart and the kids home?" Men are not known for their resourcefulness. They are inhibited by their own self-consciousness. If it is going to look funny, they won't do it. I jump inside the cart's handle and hold the handle of the cart and stroller together, taking mincing little steps. Frankie laughs. I secretly curse him because my next-to-useless husband is downtown having fun postering while I have to shop and do the laundry and his jerky friend is laughing at me, but I don't let on I am mad.

He is gleeking at me now. I can hardly wait to turn forty. Then the men my age may be less obsessed with fucking. He offers help and I take it. I have to put up with gross physical nuances like having his arm accidentally brush my breasts, but I don't care. Under the coercive pressure of hauling fifty pounds of babies and another seventy-five of groceries a full five blocks, the stupid little rubs don't seem so bad. It's his great pretence at morality, his sneakiness and his belief that I belong to my husband that really get to me. If I were to suggest we jump in bed, he would ask me about my husband; he does not think of him while he is brushing my tits, though. DING DONG.

I virtually run through the aisles, throwing things into the cart. The good behaviour mode of either of my children spans only forty-five minutes. I had wasted five precious minutes on the street talking to this fool and now they are getting restless. Screams, tears and tantrums are next.

Frankie is wheeling the cart and I am at the buggy's helm. We are moving fast. The girls love it. Columpa suddenly drops off to sleep in the middle of an incoherent bunch of babble that has a complaining tone to it. She starts swaying back and forth. Tania tries to hold her up. She is just barely managing to keep her sister in the buggy. I can't help laugh-ing.

"You look beautiful when you laugh." Too much. It is the sort of remark from a John Wayne movie—you know, he has just paddled some poor woman's backside, she's hollering falsely indignant, he says, "You know you're cute when you're mad," and then they roll around—passionately—in the hay. I wouldn't care one way or another about a tumble in the hay with this guy. Sex, love and morals have never formed a tri-umvirate in my mind, and I'm still young enough to be gleeful over doing something I am not supposed to be doing. But the line was so bad. Still, I smile full in his face, encouraging him.

Tania is nodding out. At home, I put them both to bed, lock the door and confront his amorousness. He doesn't resist. It's all so naughty and hence lovely.

"What about Tom?"

"Christ." I had forgotten that I knew he was going to say that. "How long has he been on your mind? When did you start thinking about him, when you were... "

He cuts me off. He just thought of it now.

"Well, in that case, we are all too late to do anything about it, so why don't we stop musing over hopeless things?"

The doorbell rings and I move to answer it. He grabs me and asks "what about him?" again. I wonder if some of the grey matter from his brain has sneaked out through his man-hood. Jeezuss. The doorbell again. No time to convince this twit that people come in and out of my house all the time and it isn't anybody's business which of them I sleep with, most especially not Tom's. Frankie is not dealing with this at all well. He better not make some stupid suggestion about my leaving my husband or I will beat him to a pulp.

"Tom is in jail," and Don rolls in to take a seat.

"Great. You want dinner?"

Frankie comes downstairs and is calmly greeted by our mutual friend. Frankie's face is painted with thirty different shades of guilt. I try not to think about it. It didn't go by Don;

the whole scene looks kind of funny.

"He is in jail," Don repeats himself with great patience, trying to articulate the significance of what he said.

"Yeah. I heard you. Do you want some dinner?" and I start banging the pots and pans. In 1974 I was still convinced that my whole reason for being was rooted in mothering my daughters, my husband and *his* friends. Don expected me to get all excited. What was new? He probably got drunk and landed himself in the drunk tank again.

"For postering." Well. Pardon my heresy, but that was worth at least one belly laugh. He must be the only person in Vancouver to have been charged with postering.

"It is fifty dollars to bail him out."

"Fifty dollars. Well, I just happen to have it in my ass-hip pocket. When does he go to court?"

"Tomorrow."

"He can stay there until then."

Don looks at me, a little pained. I want to say look a..hole, I do all the laundry, cook and clean after that man, type all his leaflets after midnight and mother his two children so that he can risk postering downtown. Who is in prison here? My sentence is "until death do us part"; he's going to be there overnight. I don't say it; he wouldn't understand.

In the corner, Frankie has gone catatonic with guilt. Don turns down dinner—he is miffed about my not taking the "jail in the line of duty" as seriously as I ought. In some perverse fashion he thinks that turning down a dinner invite is going to offend me. This guy believes that I cook, clean and mother because I really think it's the end-all and be-all in my life. He leaves mumbling.

"I don't know if this is right." Frankie is still bemoaning our tumble in the living room, rendered all the more disgusting for him by the knowledge that Tom was in jail while he had been helping himself to his lovely wife.

"Honey, if you are talking about morals, it was all wrong." I hear the girls scurrying around upstairs. Frankie keeps mumbling about Tom, how we shouldn't have "done it," etc., while I bang pots and pans. Boy, men are miserable. They do everything they can to get between your legs and then whine about it later. I could have hit him.

"Mahmm." My youngest is screaming and being hauled down the stairs by the oldest. She has hold of a toy that the other one is clinging to. Tania, in trying to get it away from her, is dragging the little one down the stairs. They are both crying, someone else is knocking at the door, so I put the toy on top of the fridge without bothering to tell them they can't have anything that they fight over, pick them up, coo a little, then answer the bloody door.

"C'mon in." A couple of Tom's friends come in and sit down. The conversation centres on his arrest. It's amusing. Arrested for postering. What next? I've heard that during the thirties they arrested people who made speeches without flying a Canadian flag, but this is forty years later. Maybe they'll start demanding that we get a permit to demonstrate.

"What do you say to the man? Uh, excuse me sir, but, uh, can I have permission to demonstrate against you? I mean, it's like a kid asking his mom for permission to curse the jeezuss out of her." That remark brought laughter from me only. "Not funny?" I ask, serving coffee all around.

"Bad analogy," someone mumbles.

"OK." . . . "Don't put your fingers in the butter," and I move it out of the reach of my youngest girl. "Put the hat back on his head," to the older one. "Cream, sugar?" . . . "Practically speaking, fifty bucks is a bit of a wad. I don't have it."

They seem to understand, though their faces look a little pinched. I resume cooking and someone suggests making a "run." I tell them that that is not a good plan. While Tom is home, I put up with that shit but I wasn't about to while he wasn't here. The room got a little stiff and quiet, the pair start to fidget, drink their coffee, mumble about things they have to do, then leave.

Frankie is upset. "Why'd you tell them that?"

"Because I don't want them partying in my house." I grab a diaper, change the baby, wash my hands and tend dinner.

"Don't you think it was kind of rude?"

"Yeah, that's why I told them no."

"I didn't mean *them*."

"*I* did. Pass me the cloth next to your elbow." He does. He just can't leave it alone. Somehow, he has it in his head that Tom would have let these two buy beer, drink and puke all over my house in full view of my toddlers, and while I agree he probably would have, he isn't here now and Frankie doesn't think it's OK for me to refuse them the dubious privilege of making fools of themselves in my house in Tom's absence.

"But... Tom... "

I remind him that he is not in a position to talk about what Tom allows or disallows as it was a definite given that Tom has never permitted his friends to help themselves to his wife. That hit home. He asks what we are going to do.

"We? I am cooking supper and you are sitting there waiting for it to be cooked, passing me this and that as I might require. Pass me the salt." He does. Cambie grabs it before I manage to intercept his bad pass. I have to lean into the pass and try to get it from her before she pours salt on the floor. I don't make it. It is in my hand upside down.

"These guys need a good licking."

"Yeah, I know but they are all grown up so it is kind of hard to convince them to bend over.

"I mean your daughters." Now he has really gone and done it.

"Look, sweetheart, you are really pretty and your body works the way it ought to, but father to my children you are not. Even if you were, I doubt very much that I would take your advice."

"Just look at them, they're wild." They are under the sofa playing in the box of shoes. The sofa is not really a sofa. It is two planks plunked atop four square bricks. They are too big to sit under it without raising the planks with their heads. It does look a little out of hand but they aren't hurting anyone so I don't bother telling them not to have fun. Toys they lack and if I don't let them play with whatever is at hand, I will have to run after them enforcing ridiculous prohibition laws with violence. I neither have the time nor the energy, much less the inclination.

"I never did want to be a cop, so I don't see why I ought to run around policing them." He doesn't get it. Supper is ready and I take them to the bathroom to wash up. The baby keeps trying to grab the soap, the elder is obsessed with rubbing her hands together to create bubbles and foam. I manage to rinse them off and herd them to the table.

"What about us?" Oh, good christ, here it comes again. Tania says, "what does 'what about us' mean, Mommy?" . . . "Oh, never mind, he doesn't mean anything." . . . "Then, why did he say it?" . . . "Well, what about us?" . . . "Pass the butter. Nothing." . . . "What do you mean, nothing?" . . . "Yeah." . . . "Mommy, I don't want da peez." . . . "Eat them, they're good for you," and I plunk the food into baby's mouth. "I really don't believe you, Frankie. I am married to your gawdamn friend for chrissakes." . . . "Gawdamn for chrissakes," Tania repeats the choicer words. "Well, why did you do it?" . . . "Look I did not do it by myself, number one, and number two, we both thought it was a good idea at the time." . . . "Don't put that in your hair." . . . "Pass me the rag, she put it in her hair."

"This is a gawdamn zoo."

"You better leave, Frankie." I don't need anyone calling my girls animals to their faces. I put some more food in the baby's mouth. Tania is studying her piece of meat. I tell her it's probably best to study the taste and never mind how it looks. The phone rings and I jump to answer it. The doorbell goes off and the baby stands up on wobbly legs and half crawls out of the high chair. I holler at Frankie to help her. The person at the other end of the line says "what?" Frankie is too late and I curse him. This really offends the other person. I have to hang up on her 'round about the time when she is asking me what is going on.

I figure it out while I am comforting my little girl. Frankie is all indignant that I used him. If *I* had been upset about him taking me for granted, everything would have been normal. I was supposed to be upset and shocked about what we did and he could not handle that I felt no remorse, no guilt nor any sorrow. How can one man be so many different kinds of a fool? I never did learn to act ashamed so now he was going to make me pay by picking my life apart, including attacking my parenting skills and the conduct of my children. I wanted to tell Frankie that the lady on the phone was Tom's girlfriend... that he doesn't think I know about her... Tom thinks me a fool who believes the relationship is strictly political, but I can smell her all over him when he gets home after "serving the people" with her—whatever that means. I don't say anything because he would insist that that's different.

Frankie doesn't leave. The doorbell rings again and he goes to answer it. More of Tom's friends come in. They all discuss the "politics" of Tom's arrest.

"He was probably arrested because the subject matter of the poster was South Africa," someone says.

I resume doing dishes and mothering my daughters and only half listen to the chatter. Some of it is pure theatre. It seems absurd to me to attach a whole world analysis to a simple postering charge. It never occurs to anyone that maybe cops and business people don't like their "property" smutted up with lefty posters. They act like it was part of a global capitalist conspiracy to arrest their leader, Tom. An attack on freedom of speech, at least.

"We don't have freedom of speech in this country," and I mumble out a little lesson in Canadian legalism. "Parliament is responsible to the crown, not the people; human rights, free speech, etc. are not part of our judiciary."

No one pays any attention. Patti has come over and

joined the guys in the "rap." I can't figure out why she is so acceptable to them. When she talks they respond. I find her exaggerated, rhetorical clap-trap annoying—they eat it up. I get the feeling from all of them that college kids puff up their minds in order to feel like they have some sort of meaning or universal order to their lives.

Patti has been having an affair with Tom. I don't mind that so much but I think it kind of cheeky of her to come by my house, expect me to wait on her hand and foot while she is helping herself to my husband, ostensibly behind my back. She is no ordinary woman. Most of the women who come to visit me, my friends, help with the dishes, the kids, stuff like that, while they're here. Not this one. She acts like me and the kids are dead except when she wants coffee. She has some sort of secret inside of her that inspires men to respect her brain and not intrude on her person by reducing her to a servant. I envy her position.

She holds her coffee cup up and says "thank you" to me. It's weird, but before I slept with Frankie I used to think of all this as normal. Now, I just look at her dumbly. Annoyed, she gets up and tries to pour herself a cup. The kids get in the way (perfect timing girls), and she puts the cup down. She suggests making a "run." Again, I say "no" and they all get this funny look on their faces like they're constipated. Patti asks why not.

"Because I said so." I go to the door and open it. The room empties of all the visitors except Frankie. He is not happy with the kind of person I'm becoming but he can't leave me alone. I go to put the girls to bed. Frankie sits downstairs in silence while I read them a story or two and make a couple up. At 9:00 P.M. I am lying on the sofa and Frankie mumbles that he doesn't understand me. I don't understand me either, I tell him. It seems kind of lame that I should think all of this adultery stuff a pile of cow dung, but it is what I think. I'm jealous of Patti, not sexually, but because my husband and his friends accord her her mind. I can't explain that to Frankie. I

can't tell him that she has something that I obviously lack—
something that tells all of the men around her that she is to be
taken very seriously—and that I would like to have some of
that. I sure as hell can't tell Frankie that he means nothing to
me beyond that one sexual encounter which I don't care to
repeat. What a mix-up. It's all too complicated and
inexplicable for me.

"Go home, Frankie. Tom is in jail." I roll over and face
the wall. Everything is fuzzy after that. Rolling, changing
emotions float around inside me as I lie looking at the old
hand-besmudged wall and wonder what is happening to me,
why I don't care about Tom's incarceration the way the others
do, don't feel its earth-shattering importance, and why all of a
sudden I resent them not thinking I am clever. Somehow
what I am feeling seems more important to me than Tom's incarceration, and I think they should see it that way too. The
changing emotions roar around inside, taking up speed and
intensity until fear starts to ride over it all like the surf in a
stormy sea. Panic almost overtakes me when my old granny's
face grins through the wall.

I had not seen or thought about her since the last tear I
shed just after she died a dozen years ago in our old backwoods
bush home. I hang onto the picture of her face against the
white wall I was still staring at. It calmed me some to see her.
She was telling me that confusion is just like any storm—it
rages, but at the end is the beautiful clear light of day. Stop it,
and you lock your confusion up and stay that way. Let it roll,
let it rage and she fades.

I did. I had no idea that a storm of thoughts could be so
exciting. Like a hurricane, crazy and destructive, some of it;
sometimes like a flood and at other times a tornado, but
always the thoughts and feelings were exhilarating. I don't
remember much of what I thought about—not much of it
settled down for me to hang onto, but the last thing I remember is seeing my girls and thinking, yes, they are wild. Wild,
untamed, not conquerable, and I was going to go on making

sure they stayed that way. A wicked little grin came over me while I was tossed about in the sea of my own storm, my wild little girls at my side and blessed sleep beckoning me home.

Worm

written in collaboration with Sid Bobb

All of my stories are written to entertain and teach my children. Worm is special to me because it is a synthesis of a story given to me by someone else and worked up in my own imagination. It is the story of the momentous struggle my three-year-old son had coming to grips with life and death and with the loneliness that separation from his sisters gave rise to. It took him two weeks to tell me the story. Because he knew I was a writer he kept saying, "Write this down, this is my story." The language is partly mine, partly his; likewise we share the story in its telling.

A fat, glossy, peach-coloured worm with a blue vein encircling his middle rises from the ground, pushing aside small bits of earth that cling momentarily to its sticky body, unmindful of the eyes studying him. Insistently, doggedly, he wriggles his front; middle and rear follow suit. Another inch of turf is covered.

"Worming... worming... worming along." Siddie's words come punched between cheeks squeezed by delicately clenched fists pressed hard against his face. Lips flupping out mumbled sounds at worm, who's just inching along.

"Doin' his bizness," flups through his contorted little face.

"Worming his way out of dirt bizness. Trouble must be dirty," he surmises, "dirty bizness, cuz mom always sez, 'you mustn't try and worm your way out of trouble.' Wormin' is when you move up and down and sideways but your body someways goes straight." It was for the crouched little boy a revelation, though he did not see or feel its significance. Worm showed him by doing his business.

"He is so shiny and pretty pink, nice and wigglesome. I wonder how cum big people don't likum?" Fat, pink worm stops and the tip of him worms forward to wiggle in the thin shaft of sunlight that has squeezed itself through the myriad of salmonberry leaves to the black earth below. Sunshine, so little of it gets squeezed to this corner of the yard.

The yard. The little fellow's mind, like a moving camera, travels back to the time when the yard was a tangled mass of roots and spikes he kept tripping over. Then uncle Roge, 'n' uncle Dave, 'n' Wally, 'n' Brenda 'n' Lisa 'n' Cum-pa came. Everyone was rushing around, digging and pulling roots and carrying them to where the fire was going to be, only Dennis didn't know it wasn't a fire yet, cuz he kept saying, "Take roots down to the fire." Siddie chuckles to himself at the image of his step-dad.

"That Dennis, he just kept hollering, 'take it down to the fire' and everyone took the roots to the fire." Siddie knew it wasn't a fire. It was a stick mountain, but he didn't want to hurt Dennis' feelings, so he pretended it was a fire just like everyone else. He looked up. Stick mountain is still there, a lonely sentinel watching out for the return of all the people. A great wrenching clutches his small chest, twists itself into unspeakable pain.

"Tania. . . Cum-pa," he whispers mournfully to fat worm and silent tears wash both little fists that press themselves tight at the touch of his tears. The realization that divorce has separated him from his beloved sisters falls on him with terrible force.

"The back of my hands is wet and shiny like you, fat worm. . . are you lonely too, fat worm?"

An alert, red-breasted robin from her perch in the apple tree overhead has decided the crouched figure below poses no threat to her mid-noon meal. In one graceful motion she sweeps down and snatches the worm out from under the boy's gaze.

A tiny piece of earth drops on his face, mixing with the tears that course across his cheeks to splat on his grimy hands. A scream swells from inside, gains volume, but is stopped in his throat by the picture of gold and green overhead at the centre of which a cheeping pair of gaunt babies cry out their incessant need for food. "Worm death is pain, baby birds are joy and somewhere in between wiggles loneliness." A little cloud scuttles across the sky, blocking out the brightness of nature's colours and the tears clean his cheek of earth's trace.

A large pair of hands scoop him up in their arms. He buries his face on the chest of the big guy. The soft murmurs of the man erase the remnants of the lonely scream the boy could not cry out.

Maggie

Mama worked. In the early morning hours she rose, set crab traps with our little skiff, and after breakfast she pounded them up and sometime in the afternoon she took the crabs somewhere to be sold. She came home near to our bedtime. Maggie told me she remembered the very day mama went to work for cash money. Maggie knew why too. Mama's marriage was a mess. Sometime after our dad left, she acquired a lover who didn't care much for her dependants. Maggie told me he was just a plain brute. I remember doubting her, thinking maybe it was us. All four of us were there, unwanted by our own dad, when he came. I could never see the point of wanting more from this stranger than what our own dad was prepared to give, but Maggie wouldn't hear it: "He is sick."

It was 1956. The year we got a television. Mama tried to finish work by six to watch the news. Maggie popped the corn and made tea and got the rest of us settled in to watch the show. The new black and white console stood out in stark contrast to the bare walls of our old house with its overly simplistic furnishings. An old couch and chair, an oil heater which never seemed to have any oil in it, and a brand new television. All of us lined up on the couch quietly staring at the news, none of us figuring these things really happened.

When mama was late, Maggie mocked the newscaster, filling up the broadcast with words of her own. "Anti-colonial Black movements in Africa threaten" came from the newsman, followed by Maggie's "to 'kick ass,' with white folks today." We laughed nervously. No one in our community dared used the word "white" when talking about the others. No one told us it was forbidden, but we had never heard white people referred to by anything except "them people," and always they were mentioned in hushed tones. Maggie's cheek and brass scared us. She knew something was amiss and somehow figured "kicking ass" could fix it.

After the news, Mama closed her eyes and asked Maggie to read. Mama had four books: a Bible, an unabridged dictionary and two novels, *Germinal* and *Les Miserables*. Maggie threw her heart and soul into her voice when she read, dramatizing her own passionate dream of poor people "kicking butt" with "them people." Mama never suspected a thing.

In the early morning light I would sometimes wake up and catch Maggie writing in her diary, painting with words whatever pictures of the world she wanted. Travelling to places she had not been, and imagining herself doing things she would never be allowed to do.

Sat. Dec. 10, 1956.
"Joey, Joey, Joey," an exasperated mother picked up bits and pieces of an electric train, shut off the power source and muttered softly the name of her errant son.

Joey was long gone. His little league cap plunked jauntily atop his fiery red hair, a glove in one hand, a bat over his shoulder and a softball in his ass-hip pocket. He had sauntered off to the cow field for a game with the boys.

On the little league team Joey was the back-catcher, but on the cow field he was agreeable to whatever position his mates wanted him to play. Today, he was first at bat. Tony was the pitcher and he threw Joey a dandy—WHAP! A line drive heading straight for sleepy Dave.

"Shee-it. . . chrisst. . . jeezuss," and a half-dozen bewildered boys circled Sleepy Dave, who lay peacefully motionless on the field about where the short stop ought to have been standing."

"Will ya look at the lump on his head?"

"Yeah.". . . "What a beauty," and other such mumbling carried on while Gary ran for his dad. The story ends here, because adults are not allowed in the diary.

She finished reading me her story. I asked her how come mothers were allowed in the story.

"Mothers are girls, silly, they never have to grow up." Maggie shaped me. Maybe it was what happened a little while later which made her words stick so well in my mind. What she said was true. Even the ladies from our own community called themselves girls—little girls, growing girls, old girls, but all girls nonetheless. It took twenty-four years, amid much brouhaha and some pies in the faces of a few politicians whose names I dis-remember, for me to say *women* and not girls, but it happened. It was kind of hard for me. I was among the first young females to gain adult status, and it took me a long time to figure out what being an adult entailed. Maggie must have known:

Tues., Dec. 13, 1956
"Ann, put that down. Annie for gawdsake." A firm wrist jerked the hammer from Annie's hand and the mouth who owned the hand spat out some nonsense about "gurlz, 'n' hammerz, 'n' shugger 'n' spice" and other such clap-trap Ann tried not to think about.

"Why don't you play with your Barbie doll or something, for chrissakes."

"Cuz Barbie don't drive truck and I don't like pointy tits."

The woman cursing Ann gasped, turned white and red by turns, and finally sent Ann to her room: "Until your father comes home." In her room Ann lay back and laughed about the look on Mary's face when she had found her pounding nails into the garage floor. Even more precious was her mother's look when Ann disclosed her awareness of truck driving and tits.

I was curled up into a fetal position before Maggie finished reading, terrorized by the strangeness and the boldness of her story. No one in our village mentioned tits out loud. It was like we all pretended women didn't have such things. Maggie told me tits were used to feed babies, but I had never seen the young women feed them in such a way. I dis-believed her.

*   *   *

It was near Christmas and we were busy. For catholic women Christmas means a lot of work. Mama left the crab nets to cut apples and deer heart and grind it all up with suet to make minced meat. She got us all busy candying fruit for umpteen cakes, cooking pumpkins we had grown for pies and tarts, and baking, baking, baking. For three weeks now the house would be warm and mama would be home. Mama kept up a constant chatter while we worked, spinning hilarious tales and making us all laugh. Except Maggie; she was outside chopping wood and splitting kindling or drawing oil, and she never heard mama's stories.

Dec. 15, 1956
He was here again. Loud and mean. . .

On the morning of the last day of school before the Christmas holidays Maggie was particularly quiet. She stared out the kitchen window at the beach below for what seemed like forever. The water was choppy. Choppy water meant cold. She didn't move; she just stood there watching the water thrash about. I moved up behind her, a shadow wanting bodily recognition. I watched the water and tried hard to feel what she was thinking, to see what she was seeing.

Each wave brought gallons of water forward to the shore, only to be hauled back by some invisible force to someplace no one ever saw. With all its steady movement, the ocean water never seemed to get anywhere. Odd how the movement of the waves didn't seem to have anything to do with the tide sneaking off a couple of times a day like it does.

"You see that, Stace?" The sound of her voice startled me. I didn't know she had seen me standing behind her. "There's a huge vacuum somewhere in the bowels of the ocean, sucking back the water and cutting it loose again. Regardless of the direction of the tide, the waves always seem to travel towards the shore. They are, tide and waves, as separate as a pair of divorcés with common children." Her voice took on a low, husky quality: "Mother sea is magic." She looked down at my face with the same condescending look old people use when they know they have pulled the wool over your eyes. She stroked my hair gently, put her arm around me and we both turned to watch the water for a while more. Little white caps popped up here and there—ocean snow—liquid cold. They looked like living creatures, swimming out there on the breast of the sea. Maggie groaned, wondering out loud if everyone was as pained as she was about the cold, softly whispering that they didn't seem to be.

"Do you want to eat?" The sound of mama's voice startled her just a little. Maggie once told me that when she was staring out the window like that she'd kind of go a bit deaf. Mama's voice seemed to come through a tiny hole at the end of a long tube and it was almost painful to break loose from watching the water to listen to mama.

Asking any of us if we wanted to eat was kind of rhetorical. Eating was not too regular at home, so we were always anxious to get on with it. Especially this time of year. Good catholics like we were, we sacrificed immediate eating for Christmas celebrating. Maggie was always hungry. She was the thinnest of us all. Never in all her eleven years had she ever turned down food. But it was like mama to ask. Her sense of courtesy forbade her ordering us to do anything except stop fighting.

Without answering, Maggie moved slowly towards the table. I don't think she realized she still had a hold of me. I matched my footsteps with hers and we moved to the table kind of stuck together.

She sat in silence for a long time between eating. I remember how she watched us with intense fascination, chuckling out loud at the smaller of us. The younger, fat, chubby hands grabbed at their food. They clutched their bread overzealously, mish-mashing it with their fingers, as though afraid someone might snatch food from their tender grip. The older, more competent hands held their spoons gracefully, consuming their meal with steady determination.

Maggie was always looking to see who wanted an extra bite. After our plates were empty, if one of us looked around she would spoon a little from her dish into our grateful mouths.

Most days mama would disappear amid a flurry of instructions to Maggie and a furious pace of eating, dressing and hurrying out the door to check the traps. Maggie was left to mother us. Chins were wiped, hair brushed and clothes fussed over. She readied our lunches and hollered at grampa in his cabin down below, where the littlest ones stayed till Maggie and I came home from school.

On this morning, time was running out. Maggie wolfed what food was left, reached for her jacket and we headed out the door. Her face wore a funny look of agitation. Christmas. Mama was still here. No traps to set. Maggie didn't have to take the little ones down the hill, still she hesitated a little at the door. Mama mumbled something about "looks like snow" as we set off down the street to the bus stop. Maggie's body jerked, but she never turned around to see what mama was saying.

Noon, Dec. 16, 1956
It is so cold, so cold. Not one set of hands seemed to mind getting ready to go out in the cold. I'm alone, so alone. The personal bride of cold. My insides rant and rave at the freezing rain, scream for relief from this dread of cold. This dread no one seems to share.

I have been "kept in" again. These fools have no idea their punishment is such a welcome relief. Alone, in the classroom, I am spared having to face the cold and those little brutes they call my fellow pupils, with their hideous minds who think mocking the earth-tones of my skin a great source of joy. How did they get this way?

This morning it was windy and raining a light frozen rain. It hit my face in sharp pin pricks. I hunched pathetically inside my jacket, but it didn't do a thing to keep the cold out or the warm in. I scrunched my fists into my jacket sleeves, but that too was a bit foolish. The cold crept inside, past my arms and clear to my chest. My body rattled, my walk laboured, my teeth clattered senselessly inside my head. Stacy trundled alongside of me oblivious to the cold.

* * *

Maggie had told me not long before how she hated her teachers. She held them accountable for some of her emiserating and useless struggle against the cold. They were responsible for Maggie having acquired the asinine practice of lugging home a number of unused text books, exercise books and other such stuff as hopeful teachers insisted she would need to do her homework. She wrapped the useless books in a plastic bag and tucked them under one armpit. Invariably, they slipped and fell—like mutinous little beasts they jumped out of the bag and into some puddle. The leap to the dirty water always made Maggie laugh. She refused to do her homework. The struggle escalated. She told her teachers she was not going to do it—five hours of "this boring shit" was enough for one day. Her slender hands paid dearly for such honesty.

They had been keeping her in at noon and recess and once a week the principal sought to force her hands to apply themselves more diligently to her homework by administering a few blows. She could have done without the blows, but didn't mind being kept in. She missed no one on the playground, viewed all white people as some sort of blight sent over by some wicked demon to plague us. There was not a single white person in the world whose company she would ever appreciate.

She hissed when she spoke of them. I cautioned her to try and "get along." She refused. When I told her the old people admonished us all to appreciate all human beings, she retorted that none of the old people ever had to sit next to them hour after waking hour, watching the way they looked at us. They never had to face their ignorance, their mindlessness, their loudness. No. White people are a plague of locusts sent to torment us. When she wasn't ranting about them she was laughing at their stupidity.

She and I were sitting together on the bus one day, about a mile down the road, when she laughed out loud.

"Do you know, Stace, we're still going to be studying reading and writing when we are seventeen?"

"No-o." I was horrified.

"Yeah." Persuasively she argued between giggles: "I asked yesterday. I said, 'Mrs. Jamieson, I've been studying reading for six years now, when do you suppose I will have learned it?' She sez, 'What do you mean?' so I said, 'Well, when do you stop studying reading?' Then she sez, 'You don't. In high school it's called English. You study English all through high school and if you go on to university, you study it there too.' Well, Stace, right away this numbskull says the wrong thing. I said, 'Oh and university English is for the slackers who never paid attention in high school?'

'Certainly NOT!' she sez in an offended kind of voice. Well, jeezuss, Stace, what in the world do you figure takes these people so long to learn to read the very language they claim to speak?" She laughed. It wasn't the kind of laugh you let go when you are really enjoying yourself. It was the sort of cynical laugh you let out when you find something really stupid, but hopelessly unchangeable.

It was all too much for me. I laughed. Comic relief, I

think. It didn't much matter—neither of us was going to go to university.

*   *   *

The day got colder. Later in the afternoon, the sky spilled an apron load of her largest snowflakes on the ground. Not believing sky was really going to do that, Maggie had let herself get another after school detention. I saw her leaving the classroom, her teacher shrieking "get down to the principal's office this minute," and heard Maggie yell back at her "go to hell, hag." I tried to make myself small and invisible in the hallway, as I sneaked up behind the open office door.

The principal was probably a good man, but he was always on the side of teachers—never considered the students' point of view. Bad for discipline, he must have thought. He came out of his office to where Maggie was sitting on the blue bench.

"Well, whaddaya say?"

"I hate cold." I knew it was the wrong answer. I wept from behind the door. *Don't do this Maggie,* I begged silently. *Don't be cheeky. Maybe if you said "sorry," he would let you come home.* I saw her face in my mind, her full mouth pursed in stubborn resistance. I shook in anticipation of her missing the bus. Mama never understood. She would be angry again. I could hear what she had yelled many times: "Just once, Maggie Joe, just once, you would think you could co-operate, do your damn school work and make it home on time to get your little brothers. Grampa's old. . . " I could see Maggie praying for mama to be on her side, just once. *Maggie, please hush and say you're sorry.*

"What?" the principal asked, not understanding her answer.

"I beg your pardon," she corrected him, and the world grew large for me. I shrank behind the door, leaned against the wall and sighed. *Maggie, Maggie, Maggie.* She meant no harm. In Maggie's mind no hierarchy existed. Proper English and polite presentation was demanded of her, and so she demanded the same sense of courtesy from the principal.

"You know, young lady, your impudence will not see you through life."

"I don't see why not. Your rudeness hasn't hurt you." It was the last straw. I gave up hoping and left to catch the bus alone before I missed it too. I wanted to weep for her on the bus ride home, but pride bit my lip shut. I thought about Maggie having to walk home, three-and-a-half miles by road, and wondered what went on in her mind to drive her to such madness. A little piece of me argued with my heart. *Maggie, you have got no sense. You shouldn't have done that. Why can't you do your work and just go with these people.* But my mind could not argue away the picture of Maggie, fearful of the cold, struggling to get home in the half-light of winter, dodging cars and dogs because some power hungry creep kept her in.

I couldn't stop seeing mama, incensed with Maggie's rebellious ways, and grampa, crippled with arthritis, scuttling after the little children, unable to keep up. Mama, tense, wound up tighter than a drum, hauling traps, pounding crabs, day in and day out and never making enough to feed her young. Maggie threatened our survival. She never got old enough to see that, but mama knew. Intuitively I understood it, too, in much the same way that I "knew" things Maggie thought and did.

An hour of sitting on the blue bench thinking about going home in the dark must have knocked the fight out of Maggie. When the principal let her go she mumbled a flat "thanks" without a hint of gratitude in her voice, and turned reluctantly towards the door. She paused a moment before leaving—I guess to consider asking him if she could use the phone. She must have decided the cold of the snow was warmer than the chill of having to beg, because she didn't say a thing. She left.

When I got home I offered to look after the little ones,

hoping it would soften mama's rage at Maggie's recalcitrance. They bubbled about, asking for Maggie. I told them she was still at school, for which I was battered with a whole series of "whys."

"Teacher kept her in."

"Why?"

"I don't know."

"How come?"

"I don't know." They badgered me until I told them she got a detention. They wanted to know what that was, what it looked like. Exasperated, I barked out "nevermind," which made them cry for Maggie. I turned the TV on so they could watch cartoons while I stared out the window trying to picture Maggie's way home.

Dark would have settled in by the time she left the school, bringing a mean cold. I imagined her pencil thin legs, unprotected, her little canvas running shoes soaking up the wet cold snow as she hurled her body against the wind. I pictured her hurting, hurting like a licking never could. Even the middle of her mind must have hurt. Three-and-a-half miles by road or a mile straight through the bush. I knew that dark and windy as it was, she would choose the bush, tearfully battling the cold one more time.

Sometime after four

My legs feel so thick. I don't know where I am. The wind is biting my chest. I can't drag myself forward anymore. The wind's bites have become more vicious. I tried, mama, I clawed at bushes and branches, trying to pull my thick legs along, until my hands, too, grew still with the cold. The howl of the wind is a musical call, calling me to join it. I can barely write anymore.

She sat down on a fallen log in front of a baby cedar. The sapling danced for her, and the howl of the wind became a musical call to her to join them. She bid her diary adieu. They found her, half-lying on the log, still holding the plastic bag, just a hundred yards short of the road—almost home.

Dear Diary
Have you ever felt so cold
you were warm—sleepy tired?
Happy to give up the ignorant
fight against the cold?

Please, I haven't deserted you
It's just that I am so lost
and cedar calls me, dancing,
swaying seductively. . .

* * *

Dear Maggie:
I typed out the contents of your diary and am keeping the copy.
You noted on the very first page that should anything happen to
you, the diary could be my friend. I really don't believe your
diary wants to stay in this world without you, so I am returning
her to rest with you for all eternity.

mama

Dear Diary:
When you see Maggie, tell her I love her and miss her beyond
words.

Stace

Mama and me sneaked into the church at dawn and slipped the diary (minus the first page) into the coffin holding Maggie. In the stillness of the white dawn, before the tears came, I thought I heard Maggie say, *Please Stace, little sister, tell them, tell them, I just couldn't fight the cold anymore.*

Mama sat in despondent silence for days after your departure, Maggie. Her body was at your funeral but her heart didn't believe you were really gone. Christmas came and went without celebration. On New Year's day, mama's eyes filled with water and she mumbled, "Maggie got lost, that's all there was to it. She wanted to come home, but she got lost." She rolled a cigarette and asked me to read *Germinal*, "the part where the young girl becomes a woman just at the moment of her passing." The face of Maggie danced upon the page, her last look one of panic as she wandered in a tighter and tighter circle struggling to find the road. My voice rolled out the drama of Zola's young woman, who like Maggie, had never been a child. It filled up with the steely yarn of Maggie's courage as Zola's woman-child fought for her life from the bottom of a mine shaft.

Eunice

I was just a little dry when Nora called and invited me to this meeting. I decided the gathering at Eunice's home would wet my writer's whistle. I agreed to go. There is no place for women writers, Native or otherwise, to gather together and engage in the sort of word play which would give them the endless run of story lines or unusual turns of phrases which could ignite their imaginations and help them along with their next book. For most male writers, the Austin or some other bar suffices, but as yet no one has devised the sort of coffee house with a kitchen table atmosphere to suit women writers' intellectual needs. Complicating all this is the numbers of us who have children. I am something of a fanatic on that score. With four children, I have always felt writing was a cross I chose to carry between wiping noses and throwing quick meals together, rather than a profession. A series of meetings between women had a magical appeal, even if its aim was only to organize a reading on a community radio show.

Nora had taken great pains to identify each woman and characterize them, including some of the more intimate details of their lives. Her descriptions were intended to help me understand the participants in a way that would guide how I treated them. I was familiar with all the writers but Eunice— she was agoraphobic, seriously so. She had not been out of her house for some eleven years. I didn't react over the phone, but this bit of news did spark some anxiety in me. White women, particularly writers, have changed over the past decade. In the mid-seventies, white women were still extremely defensive and ignorant about Natives. Vague recollections of really idiotic conversations nagged at me: "Why do Indian women

drink so much... why can't they look after their children...
if they are so poor, why do they continue to have large families?... " My need to be with other writers took precedence
over my misgivings about meeting with a white woman who
had not been around during the years in which those questions had been rendered inadmissible in our company. *Please,
Eunice, don't be ignorant,* I pleaded while filling my coffee
thermos and getting ready to head out the door.

I must have been late because everyone was relaxing in
Eunice's living room and sipping herb tea when I got there.
The conversation was rolling around a familiar ache in my
heart—the gnawing need for a women's and third world
writers' hang-out. Some place kitcheny and sober enough for
us to gather around and talk about works-in-progress. The
inevitable discussion about the politics of being women
writers followed. Sky, a Chinese woman struggling along with
her first novel, wondered out loud, "Why do we have to drag
ourselves through the agony of digging deeper and deeper
inside ourselves for words to paint our lives when a conversation or two with other writers would do the same trick with
much less strain and greater results?" Because women are still
islands, but I don't say that.

Eunice responds. "There is some advantage to the process of self-examination. It gives us a handle on private
truth—something you don't find much of in male writing."
Eunice's ability to write without ever leaving her home begins
to make sense. The pain of being bonded to her kitchen, the
imprisonment of domesticity and the joy of it could fill
volumes. In my silence, I don't feel so different from Eunice.
My second book was out there, folks were buying me, sticking
me on their shelves. Unlike the first time I had published, this
go round I had agreed to trot around on the usual speaker's
circuit in order to help book sales. We were both somewhat
comfortable in our feminine invisibility, only Eunice stayed
there, while I merely desired to. Each read, each performance
upset me, sometimes to the point of sickness. I cut these

thoughts short of envy for Eunice's disability.

I am lost in a kind of reverent retreat, drifting irresponsibly in and out of the conversation without helping it to focus on the project at hand, but still wearing a look of attention on my face. I am waiting for the women to climb out on the sort of tangents poets get to which could lead to my next piece. I am feeling mercenary enough to let the chatter roll in any direction it chooses. The subject isn't useful, something about yuppie food and health, so I look around and repeat the key lines of the living room. The shades of colour reflect the inner colours of Eunice's soul—warm earth tones with the odd streak of bluish grey hues all gently arranged. It strikes me as odd that the colours of autumn are comforting, not stark and painful as one might expect. Eunice's hair is warm reddish brown with streaks of grey in it. The grey matches mine in a pleasant, not fearful way.

"Were you ever encouraged to write?" Sky's emphatic "NO" jumps out at us. It about sums up the experience in the room. Women are never encouraged to write. We drift into the clothes our various types of discouragement wore. I had divorced my first husband over it.

"Drastic," someone remarks.

"Not really," I say. "My mom always wanted me to write. She would do anything to promote my writing as a child. It was almost sacred to her. While everyone was working for our common survival, she let me read or scribble. It shaped me. Made me obsessive about it. I couldn't grasp why this man failed to see my writing as more important than the damn dishes."

Sky wasn't so lucky. Her parents were concerned about her career and seeing to it that she lived a comfortable, affluent life—and writing doesn't give you that. Amazingly, she is squeezing a rewrite of her novel* between nursing shift-

---

*Disappearing Moon Café by Sky Lee, published by Douglas and McIntyre (Vancouver, B.C., 1990).

work at a hospital and single-parenting her son. Me, I would rather be poor. All but Jamila have vivid recollections of our first pieces, what happened to our early efforts, and the furious battles that burying our noses in books and dictionaries and then typing till all hours of the night gave rise to. Jamila, ever the intellectual, does not remember not writing and hence cannot remember her first piece. Her father encouraged her. Inconceivable. She has been writing since she learned to read. It was commonplace for her. Life's memories are made of the eventful not the commonplace, I note mentally, and fall back into silence.

A lull in the conversation sets in and the producer of the radio show tries to bring some order to the gathering, summing up what we have accomplished and outlining what still needs to be done. Politely, she hides how little we have gotten done behind words that make it seem like more. She has an agenda and refers to it. We appreciate this. An entire twenty-four-hour women's program has been planned for the celebration of International Women's Day. She managed to get us an hour before midnight time slot. The reading was to fit the theme "the politics of international feminism," and the group here reflected that. We all nodded. Times were discussed and some thought about who was going to introduce who was dealt with. Before she got any further down on her list of items on the agenda, I broke discipline.

"What's across the street Eunice, a school?" I am actually thinking about how dull the view must be for her, an empty gravel yard dotted with sterile box-shaped buildings isn't the stuff of great poetry. What a dense assumption that turned out to be.

"Oh that, that's my sociology project," she laughs back my surprise.

"Everyday I sit here at noon and study the students. No kidding. I have come to some interesting conclusions about teenagers. They do the same thing every day—very conservative. They stand in the same spot—very territorial. They belong to groups and always rejoin the same one—very cliquish. In fact. . . "

I leave Eunice pulling the other women into her web of story-telling and pursue my own interests. Eunice has a very typical Canadian white woman's voice with a very untypical "so glad you're here" sincerity to it. I am aware that my indigenousness never leaves the minds of white folks. I am a Native writer, never just a writer, but Eunice doesn't seem to see me that way. The paleness of her rounded face indicates a life without sun and I am thrown back to a time when I couldn't handle the world outside. I wonder what would have happened if I had stopped trying to go outside, if like Eunice I had given in to my trepidation. I recount the number of times I "came to" in some phone booth, hysteria consuming me, trying to remember my gawdamned phone number so someone could come and get me, my poor kids and my second husband taking turns talking me down enough to encourage me to leave the booth to check the street names so they'd find me. And then, the kids having to stay on the phone talking to their crazy mom while their step-dad came to get me.

I flush at the memory, then force myself to focus on Eunice again. She talks the way she looks, even round tones that float about the room without quite filling it up. I get the idea her husband plays a big role in the management of her household. I want to chuckle at the thought of this faceless man hauling kids to doctors, dentists, school field trips and parent-teacher meetings, but I don't. A piece of me wants to say how hard it must be for him. I bawl myself out. I really loathe the sympathy I can sometimes come up with when men are stuck with doing the work women consider normal living. If *he* was the disabled person I know I wouldn't feel the same way towards her. I'd be saying something dull like "she must be strong."

Just then Eunice comes up with, "My gawd, did you know there are 700 pagans in B.C.?" Out of the blue, just like that. I'm anxious to see how she intends to make sense of it.

"I was sitting at home the other night and I turned on the news channel—only an agorophobe would do such a thing—and guess who is talking direct from Holland? Our very own premier. He's saying there are only 700 pagans in British Columbia. Where are they?" Love it. We speculate about how this idiot managed to count that high and imagine him running about the province spying on the religious activities of various people, scouting out pagans and committing them to memory, and my mind returns to that other place. I can't stop cheating everyone. Nora jars me loose before I get too deep.

"Lee, did a publisher ever turn you down for reasons you felt were culturally or racially biased?" She up and stepped right into it, like I'd set her up.

"Yes."

"What was the excuse?"

"It was a story about a Native woman who had worked in a cannery and drank herself to death. They said, 'Take the drinking out and we'll buy it.' I took my story back. It is kind of hard to take the drinking out of a story about a woman who dies of alcoholism." Everyone laughs. Wicked. I was now pulling her in and playing the moment for all it was worth. Nasty.

"Who the hell was that idiot?" from Nora.

"You," I answered with feigned modesty.

"Aagh," and she fell over. "*Makera* readership was liberal. I mean the whole world could blow itself away and they wouldn't care, so long as no one talked about it. My gawd, what a payback. You know, the first lesbian story I ever wrote got exactly the same response. 'Take out the drinking.' "

The quiet got a little sticky, but not unbearable. We aren't really sure what all this means.

"Maybe they can't look at it because the invisibility they are responsible for creating is the cause of our death and they don't want to know that. Anyway, in some ways we have come a long way. We could never have laughed about such things as this fifteen years ago," I offer. We agree on that.

Eunice, meantime, is in some kind of shock.

"You're Native Indian, aren't you?"

Oh christ, here it comes, as I answer "yes" and numb up for the next line.

"How stupid of me, now I see it. I guess you get enough of that? I mean, I knew you weren't white, but... Oh, I better shut up before I get both feet in my mouth."

The stiffness in the room was palpable. It dawns on me as odd that Nora, who told me what everyone else was all about, including their racial and national heritage, had not mentioned mine to Eunice. At the same time, I am watching Eunice really intently. She looks as though she doesn't really give a tinker's damn about my race. She was surprised she hadn't seen it, was all. Only Jamila is not paying attention to the tension.

"How come women don't write about political meetings?" she asks as though the question were not new. She was lying back more like some Honolulu poolside tourist than a serious writer. Eunice mentions weakly that she doesn't go to meetings, but that she's getting ready to. The latter remark came out punctuated by a false sense of enthusiasm, while the former sounded a little guilty. Nora had prepped us about Eunice in the hope that none of us would blurt out any painful remarks like this. No one says it, but we all feel like Jam has said something out of turn. Eunice talks about her impending "coming out" ceremony—a meeting of disabled people—and we just listen. Meetings, I tell myself, serve political ends, but they are not that political. Agendas, concealed and open, tend to obscure the politics of our lives. Besides, the rhetoric that gets thrown around at meetings is really rather boring. I recall my efforts to get here, running about readying my four kids for my departure, giving last minute instructions about their care to my husband and finally robbing my change bank of loonies* so that I can buy gas on the way—that's political.

---

*colloquial term for Canadian one dollar coins.

The hint of inadequacy in Eunice's voice about the question, too, was political.

The agenda begins winding down. The producer has given up trying to keep us organized. She mentions topics for next week's discussion, including planning the logistics of Eunice's participation. Bad timing. Eunice, still raw from the political meetings question, looks uncomfortable, like her being on the show is going to be a lot of trouble. I suppose producers have a different mind set, but I can't help thinking the question was framed a great deal more importantly than was necessary. What sort of logistics do you need to plan to answer the phone? Eunice, on the other hand, presumes that anything involving an agoraphobe is bound to be troublesome, and she patiently awaits the plan. I'm embarrassed for her. I think about missing her in the studio and leave them all there while I look out on the schoolyard and imagine the stones, millions upon millions of them, each with its own grey originality. I relive Eunice's poetic, locked-in existence. I imagine her words carefully chiselled from her aspirations to chart her own course. A plain grey stone that sought her own preciousness, wanted to be alone, rather than conform to all the rest. I used to think my attendance at meetings was all so essential to my writing, but I doubt that now. At one time, I even wanted to write about the meetings. " 'This meeting is now called to order,' the chairperson pounded her gravel and the crowd slid into their seats, obediently. The loud murmurs of conversations hushed and everyone waited in anticipation for the proposed agenda to be read." As I stare hard at the schoolyard stones and imagine the cliques of teenagers gathered in the same spot and think about the cliques that gather at meetings, I am struck by the emptiness of the question.

The faces of the other women blur while Eunice's becomes clear. I want to tell her that she hasn't missed anything by not attending meetings. Her life was shaped by her desire for feminism outside the isolation of agoraphobia. At home alone, she could only remember the world as it was, and reconstruct it in the way she wished it to be. It had driven her to solitary exile and she had managed to turn the exile to account. Now she wanted out. It was a cherished goal for her. She wanted to be with other feminists. The power of her isolation, complicit as she was in its creation, escaped her. Few people possess the courage to sit in solitude with their private selves, unravel all the junk they collect by living, and then march out into the world unencumbered, with a different sense of what they might create out there. It was a goal, but I didn't believe that not attending meetings was what she really missed about not being out there.

Outside she sees teenagers and sociology and I see stones, sameness, individuality and power. The stones stretch and rearrange themselves into mountains. Hillsides, covered with huckleberries. I imagine Eunice and me trudging along the mountains of my birth, picking berries. I see the sun capture the gold and red of her hair and hear us conjure up our next poem, but I don't say a word. A brief good-bye and the meeting is over.

Yin Chin

for Sharon Lee, whose real name is Sky, and for Jim Wong-Chu

she is tough,
she is verbose,
she has lived a thousand lives

she is sweet,
she is not,
she is blossoming
and dying every moment

a flower
unsweetened by rain
untarnished by simpering
uncuckolded by men
not coquettish enough
for say the gals
who make a career of shopping
at the Pacific Centre Mall

PACIFIC CENTRE, my gawd
do North Americans never tire
of claiming the centre
of the universe, the Pacific and
everywhere else...

I am weary
of North Americans
so I listen to SKY

Standing in the crowded college dining hall, coffee in hand, my face is drawn to a noisy group of Chinese youth; I mentally cancel them out. No place to sit—no place meaning there aren't any Indians in the room. It is a reflexive action on my part to assume that any company that isn't Indian company is generally unacceptable, but there it was: the absence of Indians, not chairs, determined the absence of a space for me. Soft of heart, guilt-ridden liberals might argue defensively that such sweeping judgement is not different from any of the generalizations made about us. So be it; after all, it is not their humanity I am calling into question. It is mine. Along with that thought dances another. I have lived in this city in the same neighbourhood as Chinese people for twenty-two years now and don't know a single Chinese person.

It scares me just a little. It wasn't always that way. The memory of a skinny little waif drops into the frame of moving pictures rolling across my mind. Unabashed, she stands next to the door of Mad Sam's market across from the Powell Street grounds, surveying "Chinamen" with accusatory eyes. Once a month on a Saturday the process repeats itself: the little girl of noble heart studies the old men. Not once in all her childhood years did she ever see an old man steal a little kid. She gave up, not because she became convinced that the accusation was unfounded, but because she got too big to worry about it.

"Cun-a-muck-ah-you-da-puppy-shaw, that's Chinee for how are you," and the old Pa'pa-y-ah* would laugh. "Don't wander around town or the old Chinamen will get you, steal you, . . . Chinkee, chinkee Chinamen went down town, turned around the corner and his pants fell down," and other such truck is buried somewhere in the useless information file tucked in the basement of my mind, but the shape of my social life is frighteningly influenced by those absurd sounds. The

---

*grandfather

movie is just starting to lag and the literary theme of the pictures is coming into focus when a small breath of air, a gentle touch of a small woman's hand invites me to sit. How embarrassing. I'd been gaping and gawking at a table-load of Hans long enough for my coffee to cool.

It doesn't take long. Invariably, when people of colour get together they discuss white people. They are the butt of our jokes, the fountain of our bitterness and pain and the infinite well-spring of every dilemma life ever presented to us. The humour eases the pain, but always whites figure front and centre of our joint communication. If I had a dollar for every word ever said about them, instead of to them, I'd be the richest welfare bum in the country. No wonder they suffer from inflated egoism.

I sit at the table-load of Chinese people and towards the end of the hour I want to tell them about Mad Sam's, Powell Street and old men. Wisely, I think now, I didn't. Our sense of humour was different then. In the face of a crass white world we had erased so much of ourselves, and sketched so many cartoon characters of white people over top of the emptiness inside, that it would have been too much for us to face the fact that we really did feel just like them. I sat at that table more than a dozen times but not once did it occur to any of us that we were friends. Eventually, the march of a relentless clock, my hasty departure from college the following semester and my failure to return for fifteen years took its toll—now even their names escape me.

Last Saturday—seems like a hundred years later—was different. This time the table-load of people was Asian and Native. We laughed at ourselves and spoke very seriously about our writing. "We really believe we are writers," someone said, and the room shook with the hysteria of it all. We ran on and on about our growth and development, and not once did the white man enter the room. It just seemed too incredible that a dozen Hans and Natives could sit and discuss all things under heaven, including racism, and not talk about white people. It had only taken a half-dozen revolutions in the third world, seventeen riots in America, one hundred demonstrations against racism in Canada and thirty-seven dead Native youth in my life to become. I could have told them about the waif, but it didn't seem relevant. We had crossed a millennium of bridges over rivers swollen with the floodwaters of dark humanity's tenacious struggle to extricate ourselves from oppression, and we knew it. We had been born during the first sword wound that the third world swung at imperialism. We were children of that wound, invincible, conscious and movin' on up. We could laugh because we were no longer a joke. But somewhere along the line we forgot to tell the others, the thousands of our folks who still tell their kids about old Chinamen.

* * *

It's Tuesday and I'm circling the block at Gore and Powell trying to find a parking space, windows open, driving like I belong here. A sharp, "Don't come near me, why you bother me?" jars me loose. An old Chinese woman swings a ratty old umbrella at a Native man who is pushing her, cursing her and otherwise giving her a hard time. I lean towards the passenger side and shout at him from the safety of my car: "Leave her alone, asshole."

"Shuddup you f.ck.ng rag-head." I jump out of the car without bothering to park it. No one honks; they just stare at me. The man sees my face and my cowichan, bends deeply and says sarcastically that he didn't know I was a squaw. Well, I am no pacifist, I admit: I belt him, give him what for, and the coward leaves. I help the old woman across the street, then return to park my car. She stays there, where I left her, still shaking, so I stop to try and quell her fear.

She isn't afraid. She is ashamed of her own people—men who passed her by, walking around her or crossing the street to avoid trying to rescue her from the taunts of one of my people. The world rages around inside me while she copiously describes every Chinese man who saw her and kept walking. I listen to her in silence and think of me and old Sam again.

Mad Sam was a pioneer of discount foods. Slightly over-ripe bananas (great for peanut-butter-and-banana bannock sandwiches), bruised apples and day-old bread were always available at half the price of Safeway's, and we shopped there regularly for years. I am not sure if he sold meat. In any case, we never bought meat; we were fish-eaters then. I doubt very much that Sam knew we called him "Mad" but I know now that "mad" was intended for the low prices and the crowds in his little store, not for him. In the fifties, there were still store-owners who concerned themselves with their customers, established relationships with them, exchanged gossip and shared a few laughs. Sam was good to us.

If you press your nose up against the window to the left of the door you can still see me standing there, ghost-like, skinny brown body with huge eyes riveted on the street and the Powell Street grounds. Sometimes my eyes take a slow shift from left to right, then right to left. I'm watchin' ol' Chinamen, makin' sure they don't grab little kids. Once a month for several years I assume my post and keep my private vigil. No one on the street seems to know what I'm doing or why, but it doesn't matter. The object of my vigil is not appreciation but catchin' the old Chinamen in the act.

My nose is pressed up against the window pane; the cold circles the end of my flattened nose; it feels good. Outside, the window pane is freckled with crystal water drops; inside, it is smooth and dry, but for a little wisp of fog from my breath. Round o's of water splotch onto the clear glass. Not perfectly round, but just the right amount of roundness that allows you to call them o's. Each o is kind of wobbly and different, like on the page at school when you first print o's for teacher.

I can see the rain-distorted street scene at the park through the round o's of water. There are no flowers or grass in this park, no elaborate floral themes or landscape designs, just a dozen or so benches around a wasteland of gravel, sand and comfrey root (weeds), and a softball backstop at one end. (What a bloody long time ago that was, mama.)

Blat. A raindrop hits the window, scrunching up the park bench I am looking at. The round *o* of rain makes the park bench wiggle towards my corner of the store. I giggle.

"Mad Sam's. . . Mad Sam's. . . Mad Sam's?" What begins as a senseless repetition of a household phrase ends as a question. I know that Mad Sam is a Chinaman. . . Chinee, the old people call them—but then, the old people can't speak goot Inklish. But what in the world makes him mad? I breathe at the window. It fogs up. The only kind of mad I know is when everyone runs aroun' hollering and kicking up dust.

I rock back and forth while my finger traces out a large circle which my hand had cleared. Two old men on the bench across the street break my thoughts of Sam's madness. One of them rises. He is wearing one of those grey tweed wool hats that people think of as English and associate with sports cars. He has a cane, a light beige cane. He half bends at the waist before he leaves the bench, turns, and with his arms stretched out from his shoulders flails them back and forth a few times, accentuating his words to the other old man seated there.

It would have looked funny if Pa'pa-y-ah had done it, or ol' Mike, but I am acutely aware that this is a Chinaman. Ol' Chinamen are not funny. They are serious, and the words of the world echo violently in my ears: "Don't wander off or the ol' Chinamen will get you and eat you." I wonder about the fact that mama has never warned me about them.

A woman with a black car coat and a white pill box hat disturbs the scene. Screech, the door of her old Buick opens. Squeak, slam, it bangs shut. There she be, blonde as all get out, slightly hippy, heaving her bare leg, partially constrained by her skirt, onto the bumper of her car and cranking at whatever has to be cranked to make the damn thing go. There is something humorously inelegant about a white lady with spiked heels, tight skirt and a pill box hat cranking up a '39 Buick. (Thanks, mama, for having me soon enough to have seen it.) All of this wonderfulness comes squiggling to me through a little puddle of clear rain on the window. The Buick finally takes off and from the tail end of its departure I can see the little old man still shuffling his way across the street. Funny, all the cars stop for him. Odd, the little Chinee boy talks to him, unafraid.

Shuffle, shuffle, plunk of his cane, shuffle, shuffle, plunk; on he trudges. The breath from the corner near my window comes out in shorter and louder gasps. It punctuates the window with an on-again, off-again choo-choo rhythm of clarity. Breath and fog, shuffle, shuffle, plunk, breath and fog. BOOM! And the old man's face is right on mine. My scream is indelicate. Mad Sam and mama come running.

"Whatsa matter?". . . "Wah iss it?" from Sam and mama respectively.

Half hesitating, I point out the window. "The Chinaman was looking at me." I can see that that is not the right answer. Mama's eyes yell *for pete's sake* and her cheeks shine red with shame—not embarrassment, shame. Sam's face is clearly, definably hurt. Not the kind of hurt that shows when adults burn themselves or something, but the kind of hurt you can sometimes see in the eyes of people who have been cheated. The total picture spells something I cannot define.

Grandmothers, you said if I was ever caught doing nothing you would take me away for all eternity. The silence is thick, cloying and paralyzing. It stops my brain and stills my emotions. It deafens my ears to the rain. I cannot look out to see if the old man is still there. No grannies come to spare me.

My eyes fall unseeing on a parsnip just exactly in front of my face. They rest there until everyone stops looking at my treacherous little body and resumes talking about whatever they were talking about before I brought the world to a momentary halt with my astounding stupidity. What surprises me now, years later, is that they did eventually carry on as though nothing were wrong.

The floor sways beneath me, while I try hard to make it swallow me. A hand holding a pear in front of my face jars my eyes loose from the parsnip.

"Here," the small, pained smile on Sam's face stills the floor, but the memory remains a moving moment in my life.

* * *

The old woman is holding my hands, saying she feels better now. All that time I wasn't thinking about what she said, or speaking. I just nodded my head back forth and relived my memory of Mad Sam's.

"How unkind of the world to school us in ignorance" is all I say, and I make my way back to the car.

Dear Daddy

I am going to be fourteen next month. I am almost grown up now, so I thought you might like to know what kind of a child I am before I am not one anymore. I know you don't know very much about me because I could never tell you—you weren't there to tell. Oh, I understand you tried to be there, daddy, but it just couldn't happen. I know it wasn't your fault. Still, I thought you might want this letter to help you see the kind of girl I have been without you.

I am not very tall, about five feet, my hair is long and mommy says I am pretty—but that's how love-eyes see. I am honey-brown, amber coloured. I never see girls like me on billboards, but I don't mind, most of them aren't modest.

Do you remember when I was three? No? Well me and you got lost. We were out with your friends. The big people, you, Mary and her man, were drinking. You got drunk, you argued with the taxi driver and he threw us out and then you punched him. Sister and I and Mary were scared. We all took off and then you and I played that game. Damn game. We were walking in front of Mary and sister—at least we thought we were in front—and you said "let's hide." They disappeared. We couldn't find them. It got cold and dark and you kept asking me where our street was. I knew the name but couldn't read the signs. We both started to cry. It was the first time I made you cry.

Mommy was trying to have another baby and wasn't happy with sister and me—maybe that was why she wanted a new one. We were both bad. She yelled, "Go to bed," a lot and then she would talk through her teeth. "You are going to go to bed, gawdammit," and she would spank us with the wooden spoon. We were scared when she was so mad. All that hate in her eyes. We would beg her not to hit us, especially me, because sister would always get in bed before she came with the spoon but I would get hit.

"Bend over," she would yell. I would dance up and down and around begging "Please, please, no, mommy, no-o, no-o, no-o."

"If you don't bend over I am going to hit you anywhere I can." Then I would run all over the room, over the bed and around the chair trying to get away from her. She hit me all over. All the while I would beg "Mommy, I'll be good, mommy, I love you, mommy, please, no, no, no." I didn't mean to be bad. I just couldn't get into bed, so busy was I with trying to get away from the damn spoon. Finally, I would fall on the bed screaming, she hitting me all over until she got tired. You don't remember, daddy, because you weren't there. I think mommy thought you weren't there because of her. Was it us, daddy? Was it because you didn't like us to be bad?

Sister told mommy she hated her. I know why. Mommy cried and cried. That was the end of the winter she hit us. She still yelled at us, but when she started yelling she would suddenly stop and go to her room, like she thought she was bad. Sometimes she yelled at you. Once she threw milk on you. Yelling like she was full of hate. I know you don't remember, but I can see her now, yelling at your lifeless form on the couch, your old newspaper covering up your face and your feet.

Then she had her baby and he took up most of her time. She started to leave us alone more. He was so tiny and kind of helpless looking. He couldn't laugh or play or anything. Mommy laughed more. Just once, though, I saw her lying down looking up at the ceiling like she was dead. She couldn't hear me when I asked her as nice as I could about supper for sister and me, so I learned to cook.

We both were going to school then and I wasn't so lonely. Before the baby I had to go to kindergarten for awhile. The kids called me names and I got into fights and mommy said I didn't have to go anymore. She had such a faraway sadness in her eyes, and then she hugged both sister and me for a long time. She didn't make a sound, but I could feel the wet against my hair from her tears. After, she made tea and told us little funny stories about four bratty little kids and we all laughed.

Sister quit kindergarten too. The teacher made her sit in a corner every day for three weeks because she didn't have carrots and celery, just peanut butter—sister liked peanut butter. It got on the carpet and sister got into trouble. Mommy went to the school and the teacher started to yell at her. Mommy squared off, hands on her hips, and bellowed right back. You remember, mommy has a big voice for such a little person. The teacher started to talk nice, but sister still refused to go to school and mommy took her home. Even after the teacher said sorry, sister never went back. I was lonely again.

Mommy yelled at other people, once at a guy driving a car that almost ran us over. He got out of the car, but she wasn't scared. I think she could have beat him up, but he got back in the car. Another time someone pushed her and the baby; she hollered and pushed right back. She handed me the baby first, of course. I wonder if these men are ashamed to be so afraid of such a small woman.

It was around then that I learned about "can't afford this and that." We were on welfare, you see, daddy, and mommy was sneaking and going to school. Welfare wasn't supposed to find out or mommy would get into deep trouble. We were kind of proud of her, going to school, looking after us and trying to fix everything so she could get a good job and me and sister and baby would never have to have "fast days" again. Did I forget about "fast days"? Every end of the month we would run out of things like food and mommy talked about the old days when our "people"—she always says "our people"— used to fast and clean out their system. We didn't mind.

The welfare found out about school and mommy got cut off. She looked thinner and sadder. She just said she would have to find a job sooner than she wanted to, and she did.

The people next door moved away. We were the last kids on the block and we had no one to play with after school except each other. It was hard, now that mommy was working. I had to get sister ready for school and she wouldn't listen too well to me. I'd have to say over and over "Come on now, eat your cereal, c'mon now, put your boots on," and like that until finally she'd be ready. She still sang then, daddy, like a little bird. I forgave her not getting ready because she sang to me the whole time I was cooking mush and putting her socks and shoes on. Mommy kept warning her, "You are old enough to remember this. When you are seventeen, little lady, you will be embarrassed at not dressing yourself when you were seven years old."

Work must have been good for mom because although she always seemed to be hurrying, she laughed and treated us better. She stopped being so sad and she never looked out the window for you anymore. I asked her if she was ever going to bring home a boyfriend. "What for?" she said. "I got all the friends here I need. I sure don't need another round of misery." I didn't understand her. I thought she meant she didn't miss you, daddy, and I was scared. How could she not miss you? Sometimes I had bad dreams. I would dream the welfare took us away and no one missed us, not even mommy. Daddy where were you?

We put holes in our ceiling with our umbrellas and then we were scared of the mice falling through the holes. We had it coming, I guess—we were naughty to put those holes in the ceiling. Anyway, mommy said, "It's your own damn fault, now go to bed." Not loud, she said it kind of cool. It took me such a long time to stop crying and finally fall asleep. I knew better than to make noise—just tears trailing down my cheeks and sister's soft deep breathing, the dark and my crazy imagination working overtime, whispering evil about you and the mice.

Morning always came though. I don't remember when I

first noticed that. One morning mommy was singing in the kitchen. I realized it was the first time I had heard her sing in a long time.

"Do I look any browner?" she asked.

"No-o," I answered soft and slow, wondering what the heck she was up to.

"I am an Indian now." She said it as though it were something you could become, and I began to think she was really losing it. She went through a whole bunch of explaining about Bill C-31. I hear that line a lot since she got her "status back." Bill C-31. You know when you are ten, Bill C-31 sounds like the name of some kind old man who runs about fixing things for Native women. What did it all mean? Well, it meant mommy could go to school and we never had "fast days" again. Finishing her degree was a lot of pain for her. She wasn't young and learning didn't come so easy as it used to, she said. She wept through math, physics and chemistry, and didn't do too bad in English. When she was almost a teacher she told us that as soon as she got her degree we would move out of the city. Then you wouldn't know where we were, daddy. Didn't you want to know, daddy, or was it all too painful being married to my mom?

Baby knew by then that you weren't coming back. He still looked out the window every now and again and asked if you are at "wirk" and when were you coming home, but not even he believed his question anymore. We all thought if we were good you would just walk right in the door again. I think about that now—the long periods of time between your coming home, mommy telling us you were out working and eventually we would learn that you were just gone, "pulling a disappearing act." You laughed when you said that. It wasn't funny, daddy.

I started to grow up the other day, daddy. I realized that even when you were home you weren't really there. You were a body on the couch. I know now that you and mommy had not slept together since the baby, but you took three years, three painful years of going and coming—us not knowing when or if you were going to return—to actually leave. Every old Ford baby saw, he would run after it hollering "Daddy, daddy, come home," and he would cry. Mommy would bite her lip and we would all go home and hug each other. She played "Pretty Brown" hundreds of times for us the first couple of years after you went. And sister, she stopped singing. It was the one thing you really loved, we all loved. I didn't dare ask her about it. She didn't need to feel bad about not doing it on top of losing the joyful reason she did it for in the first place. Daddy, she sang because it was the one sure-fire way of making you smile. Daddy, I never saw you laugh and I would like to see you bend your head back the way mommy sometimes does and really let out a gut-busting laugh.

Time muddled along for us over the years and I am sitting here at the window of our own home (mommy bought it not so long ago) watching the ground break up and spring struggle to push back winter. There is a lonely little crocus looking up at me from her purple and yellow blossom, winking, as I write this letter. Time closed in on me like a fine, fine rain. The world got smaller and I don't remember when it happened. I peeked at the world through a thin veil full of small holes. The veil lifted and I realized flowers bloom in spring, die before fall; trees shed leaves every autumn to sleep during winter and somehow this all has to do with the greatness of the world. I can touch the greatness, feel it, and as I write this letter the unhappy feelings that were so large when I started have grown small.

I realized just now that despite all the lonely nights of tears and missing you, in the day we laughed, we ran, we jumped, we did schoolwork, and it was only in those few moments just before sleep that we thought of you and missed you. We carried on living. All this time I had written sad feelings onto my dreams just before I slept, when really, daddy, I grew up without you. I don't suppose you ever had to deal with missing us. I know now why you were always on the couch buried under a newspaper at nine o'clock at night. Mommy still won't talk about it, but I know, and it's OK. You see, daddy, you are the one to be pitied. I don't think you can laugh at your own folly, overcome weakness or see a little crocus on the lawn and imagine it winking at you.

love always,

your daughter

Polka Partners, Uptown Indians and White Folks

As a petulant youth, it never ceased to amaze me how we could turn the largest cities into small towns. Wherever we went we seemed to take the country with us. Downtown—the skids for white folks—was for us just another village, not really part of Vancouver. We never saw the myriads of Saturday shoppers battling for bargains, and the traffic went by largely unnoticed except to watch out not to get hit when crossing against the light. Drunk or sober, we amble along the three square blocks that make up the area as though it were a village stuck in the middle of nowhere.

I was part of the crowd sliding along the street towards the park. A hint of wind laced the air. Six leaves curled around crazily just above the sidewalk. Old Mose was leaning against the mailbox chuckling at the same leaves. It was fall. Old Mose had that wistful look on his face—he was thinking about home, missing it. The colour of earth death, the scent of harvest amidst the riot of fire colours, like a glorious party just before it's all over—earth's last supper is hard to deal with in the middle of the tired old grey buildings of the downtown periphery. I can see the mountains of my home through the cracks between the buildings that aren't butted one up against the other. It seemed a little hokey to take a bus across the bridge and haul ass through nature's bounty, so I don't do it anymore.

"Say," Mose almost straightened up in a subtle show of courtesy meant for me. I laughed before he said anything funny.

"You still holding up that ol' mailbox? I thought I left you here yesterday leaning on the same box." Mose laughed and told me he was just keeping it company till Tony came out of the store.

"What's he doing at the tailor's? Don't believe I ever saw one of us going in there before."

"His sister is getting married. He's buying a new shirt."

"Well, hell, must be his favourite sister. Turning the old one inside out was good enough for the last one who got foolish like that." Tony comes out of the store grinning from ear to ear, proudly displaying a brand new bag.

"First time I ever bought something no one ever wore before." We examine his new clothes without taking anything out of the bag and head in the direction of the café. Every urban reserve has its café. In Vancouver it was the 4-Star, but it could have been the Silver Grill in Kamloops or any small, Chinese-Canadian café in any other city that was clean, plain, a little worn-looking and with food about the same. Jimmy the waiter likes us and the manager doesn't like anybody.

We don't go there to eat much more than a plate of fries, a cup of tea or some wonton soup. We talk, laugh and behave like we were visiting our neighbours rather than dining out. When the bill comes we all dig in and put our collective cash on the table hoping it adds up. Once we were a few cents short. The manager was about to give it to us and Jimmy slipped in the nickel. We gave it back to him about six months down the road. Jimmy tried to make a joke about "interest" but we didn't get it, which made him laugh all the harder and like us even more.

"Oh shit." In the park across from the café some guy was bent over another guy cleaning out his wallet. Tony and I broke into a run.

"Hay-ay." The roller tried to bolt but I ran him down, thoughtlessly scolded the purveyor of the passed-out man's purse before I relieved him of his catch. Tony standing behind me must have geared up my mouth. I peaked inside the wallet—there was a whack of cash in there. I looked at the victim: a pricey leather jacket, wool slacks, gloves, Italian shoes and long black hair. He was an uptown Native, slumming, I guessed. Without feeling anything about what I was thinking, I wondered where all these uptown Natives are coming from, and pulled out a couple of twenties and handed it to the thief. He thanked me and took off.

Tony looked askance at me and asked if we should wake him up, like he thought it would be a good idea to just leave him. Mose grunted something about how he looked like your regular tourist. I gave them one of my *c'mon you guys, he's one of us* looks and moved to the bench he almost sat on. A few slaps and a pinch on the sensitive part of the neck brought him around. He grunted like a bear coming out of hibernation and sat up on one elbow, nearly falling off with the effort. I didn't recognize the booze he was drinking, must be some kind of fancy liquor I didn't know about. I leaned into his face to identify his tribe.

"My granny what big teeth you have," he said, squinting up at me between glances to the left and right. His hand reached for his hip.

"It ain't there," and he sighed without swearing. I handed him his wallet.

"You didn't steal my wallet just to shame me, so someone else must have taken it and you retrieved it—correct?" Every syllable fell out of his mouth clear and accentless.

"Where are you from?"

"Isn't it customary in Vancouver to begin with hello and how are you, maybe what's your name, before collecting vital statistics?" The arrogance I recognized, but I couldn't put together the words to answer his question. Vancouver had become a collector of Natives from all over. Where you were from determined how we treated you in some way I couldn't explain, so I ignored what he said.

"You're bigger than most but you don't look prairie, so you must be from Ontario."

"That too. Where am I?"

"Pigeon Square. Where are your glasses?"

"Huh?" and the blast of unfresh booze made me step back.

"Your glasses."

"Now that is twice in a row you have identified two facts of my life without ever having seen me before. You are a clever little girl, did you know that?" He was upright and looking at me different, studiously, I think. A small crowd gathered behind me.

"Wrong two out of three. I am clever, but I am not little or a girl. This must be the first time you been here." Titters from the crowd.

"Bingo." His mouth formed a perfect smile, white teeth even and well cared for. He is beginning to look like a polka partner from the other side of the tracks that form my colour bar. As I walk away, Tony is wearing a smug grin and Mose is chuckling. Polka boy knows he's been told off. He's European enough to imagine he was getting somewhere, but Indian enough to know he's blown it. He doesn't look all that confused.

Mose jumps into small talk like there hadn't been any interruption in our conversation. "So Frankie bought a new car." We laugh. Frankie has owned and junked a perpetual run of cars but none of them could ever have passed for new. We get all caught up in laughing about the aging symptoms of all the cars he ever bought. Polka boy recedes into the train of Frankie's cars and their missing parts that grew in Frankie's yard like a graveyard. I am already slipping away from the laughter and dreaming of Frankie and home and thinking he stays on our little reserve just so he can keep the train of wrecks coming or else he'd have joined us on this side long ago.

Frankie is inside the café surrounded by the regulars and bragging about his Salish Cadillac. "Not a damn thing wrong with it, talked him into lettin' it go for twenty-five bucks."

"Did the chauffeur come with it?" and everyone cracks

up. The conversation rolls around the parameters of our village and the odd or funny stories about the people in it. I stop listening and think about polkas and Prince George and the only Indian conference I ever went to. Everyone there had been uptown, dressed in the Sunday best of white folks. It surprised me at the time. The music was the same, but the people were like the man in the square. They pinched out their words pronouncing every single letter and whistling out their s's as though they were all terrified about saying fis' instead of fish. The polka music brought out the risqué side of me and despite my better judgement, I had opted for a mattress thrash with some guy.

It was like tying on a good one. The morning after sharpened the loneliness. I guess loneliness is the mother of all promiscuity, because here I was thinking of doing it again— only now the body had the face of the man in the park. It shook me a little. I reached into my pocket, calculated my share of the food costs and wondered if I had a free quarter. The banter at the table took on a slippery quality. I couldn't focus on the faces. My hand toyed with the quarter and of its own accord put it to rest in the folds of my pocket.

*   *   *

Time crawled by all winter. I spent most of it staring at my hills just across the water, watching snow woman dress them up in white and wishing I was lost there. Every now and then I'd venture out to the old café, but polka boy seemed to spend a lot of time there. His dress code and language never changed, but he did learn to turn the volume of his arrogance down enough to grow on everyone. He was at the 4-Star talking up this "centre" he wanted to create. He captivated the imaginations of the regulars. I am not sure whether it was him that scared me or his centre. No one here dreamed dreams like that. Life here is raw, wine is drunk not because it is genteel, but because it blurs, dulls the need for dreams, knocks your sense of future back into the neighbourhoods for whom it works—white folks.

I stared out of my window at the street below as though somehow my eyes would screw out from the sidewalks the words to describe my feelings. Why the hell did anyone want a centre, an office? We had the café. It was a hangout for those of us not quite cognizant of the largesse of the city, but aware we were not truly alone. Bridge Indians. Not village, not urban. An office is urban. Somehow Jimmy the waiter, the cranky manager and their café kept us just a little village. It was a place where we could locate our own in any city. Like an urban trail to the local downtown village. This guy wanted to sever the trail.

I scribbled little notes to myself. . . *"the Silver Grill in Kamloops, the 4-Star in Vancouver, Ken's Café someplace else. . . An office is not a hang-out."* Scribbling didn't help and I took to the wine bottle. In those days I didn't have much re-spect for my private words. The blur of the wine and the rhythm of country music and Patsy Cline crying in my living room didn't do much either. After a while the blur became stark, the pictures stayed real. What got blurry was my capa-city to think about it, to see my way out, and that got un-bearable too, so I left it behind. I was feeling like I needed to see my way out even if it was only a dream when I stumbled into the café.

I had been holed up for a while. I joined Frankie's table. Aside from his penchant for buying old cars he also served up his own kind of journalism. He ran down the news. . . Rufus had sobered up in great anticipation of the centre and making the village more respectable. . . Polka boy was soon to rent an office and some Métis woman was going to be the secretary. I tried not to encourage such talk. You don't need hope to cloud your life either. I stayed long enough for Tony to tease me about how I looked as though my best friend had died and everyone chided me for being a stuck-up hermit.

Outside spring had sneaked up on my world. Spiky slivers

of earth-milk squeezed from her voluptuous breasts streaked across my face. I imagined the crocus flowers of home forcing their way through these sidewalks and trees, buds upturned, lining the dingy street. A frightful clatter of bumping, grunting and laughter from a group of villagers and my almost-polka-partner right there in the thick of it all broke my reverie. They were actually moving into a little storefront on the drag. I followed the racket inside. Everyone who had a sense of stability for our sorry little half-village was there, save Tony and Frankie. It was polka boy's community centre/street patrol come to life.

I could barely stay on my feet. The room pulsed with movement and the people receded. My imagination ran on about the reality of it, arguing with the impossibility of it surviving. I saw the street, its frail dark citizenry rushing pell-mell towards this dream and imploding at the end of the dream's arrest. For arrest it would. No one would allow the total transformation of this end of town into a real community. Its attraction, its magic lay in remaining a peripheral half-village that could accommodate sentinels—not people, but sentinels, alone on a bridge, guarding nothing.

My smile hardened itself onto the line of my face while my insides cried in silence. My words, empty of content, fell in broken shards to the floor before they reached the faces they were aimed at. Nonsense greetings, mumbles of "how are you" dropped unanswered. They were busy. Every lousy piece of furniture—the old black telephone, file cabinets, coffee makers and cups—was carefully hauled in as though it was the finest possession these poor folks had ever seen.

I pretended to be caught in the wonder of it all. "Here, put the desk over there, no here, plug the phone in, couches over there," and soon I was in the centre of it, as though it had been my idea all along. It was a star-quality performance for an Indian who would never see Hollywood. I kept it up all through the move. At home later Tony and Frankie's faces haunted me. It occurred to me that they had been sitting at the back of the café alone for the first time. Tony didn't buy the dream and Frankie had no interest in dreaming for the folks down here. He had never left our reserve.

I stopped dropping by Tony's place for the regular tea and laughter while I wrestled with joining the gang at the centre or stubbornly clinging to the old café. It took a couple of months, but I did join the ranks of staff and volunteers who manned the office and conducted the street patrol. The office: it never struck anyone as hilarious at the time, at least no one laughed out loud, but the office was about as unofficial as it could be. One dingy little storefront on the drag, with its unwashed windows, worn linoleum and walls that sorely wanted finishing. The desk we had was not quite old enough to be antique but worn enough to be a joke, and the file cabinet needed a wrestler's touch to use. It had all been furnished by people who had bought their furniture second hand and had made a good deal of rugged use of it before handing it to us. But it was ours and we had never had a storefront that we could enter, have coffee and get treated like real customers.

We had a real secretary who hauled our butts across the fields of office life in the other world. She was appalled by our office and the nature of our work, but by and by she got used to it. Her first day would have been a major disaster had we noticed anything amiss, but naive as we were we didn't pay attention to her wool suit and high-heeled shoes or the cloying scent of her perfume. She coached us in filing, telephone reception and office politeness, though she could never get us to stop asking people if they were related to so-and-so from such-and-such if the name sounded familiar.

She came in one day full of her office etiquette and told us the mayor was coming. A hubbub of questions sprang up. "Who is the mayor anyway? what does he do? why is he coming here? when?" without regard to answers. She shut us all up, then told us what to say to sound smart without giving anything away. She ended the lesson with "and don't ask him about his relatives."

Old Rufus was best at it. He had had a lot of experience as a kid with tourists in his West Coast island home. He and the other kids had learned to small talk while they fleeced them of whatever quarters they could get. The mayor loved him. Edmonds came in shortly after the mayor's arrival. The press was there and the place was a general zoo. I was squeezed up in the corner. I knew enough about who the mayor was to stay in my corner. He was head of police and that was enough for me to have nothing to say. Edmonds puffed up his chest, asked the mayor if he liked Edmonds' clean suit. The mayor said a constipated sounding "why yes," and Edmonds was on a roll.

"How is your grandmother?"

"She's dead."

"Too bad, mine too... mmm, mm... and where are you from?"

"I am from Kitsilano," and Edmonds corrected him. "I mean, where are your grandmothers from, what part of Europe?" ... and the secretary grabbed the mayor and pointed to the statistical breakdown of newly employed youth, etc.

Ol' Edmonds didn't catch on to the coaching and the secretary had a few laughs about that later. "How is your grandmother?" and she would bust up. Defensively, Rufus pointed out that it must have cost Ol' Edmonds five bucks to clean his suit. It was the first time I ever saw an Indian laugh at how we are and Rufus felt it too. I couldn't put my finger on it then, but it occurs to me now that Edmonds was something like our unelected chief. He was the one we all went to to settle disputes or claim the dead. She shouldn't have laughed.

Polka boy was our boss and he spent more time at a place called head office than he did down at the storefront. Everything was going so fast. I got to be friends with the secretary who took me uptown every now and then, showed me the other places she had worked. Great anonymous buildings, filled with women who sat behind desks in assembly line style banging out pieces of paper with weird words on them like accounts receivable, correspondence, budget reports and such. A couple of times we went in. She chatted with the women about everything from the new technology to new hairdos. When they laughed they seemed to hold the laughter in the way a kid squeezes air out of a balloon so as to make just a little squeaking sound. It all felt so bizarre.

Then I was beginning to feel weepy, like there was something being born inside and growing of its own will—a strange kind of yearning. The tears began to possess a beginning, an end and a reason for their growth. Although I didn't really want to know, it came anyway, flash-flood style. As the mystery of office work fell away from these women, the common bond of survival was replacing my former hostility. The sea of white faces began to take on names with characters.

It was around this time that the doctor came. She wanted to start this clinic and was asking us to help. Us? Help a doctor? I plugged my laughter with "What do you want us to do?"

"First, I am a lesbian feminist."

"Is that a special kind of doctor?" The secretary and polka boy both laughed. I wished I had gone to school past seventh grade.

"She's gay," the secretary translated.

Thick silence followed. We didn't quite know what to do with the information. Some hung their heads like they'd rather not know. I wasn't sure what this had to do with the question... did she want us to help her find a woman?... change her mind? I knew better than to ask. I looked at the boss, the guy who gathered us here in the first place. He was studying me intently. He slowly re-positioned himself before speaking. I had the feeling that he had set this up. She didn't need us to help, she needed him and he wouldn't move without all of us and somehow he thought I was the key to getting everyone else's co-operation.

He went into a monologue about the number of accidents, the deaths of our people on their way to the hospital or in the emergency room and patiently painted a picture of racist negligence for us. A clinic with a friendly doctor would assure proper immediate care. *Where the hell is all this going?* I didn't say that, I just looked away like the rest. I guess he decided to gamble on our assent because at the end he just said, "We can't promise you won't get abuse from some of the street people, if that is what you are asking. We can guarantee the staff here won't bother you. We don't care who sleeps with who."

Oh gawd this is going to be a mess. We all knew one of the guys was gay. We also knew he had to hide this fact from some of our lovely clientele. We further knew that he had never publicly admitted it to any of us. It was an open secret. We all side glanced him. He stared catatonically off into space.

The meeting was over, chairs were put away and I got ready to go out the door. A hand tapped my shoulder and the boss called me aside. In the little walled-in space behind the store front he asked me what I thought.

"That you're about the densest Indian I ever met."

"Why?"

It was too hard to tell him that white people cannot deal with the beauty in some of us and the crass ugliness in others. They can't know why we are silent about serious truth and so noisy about nonsense. Difference among us, and our silence, frightens them. They run around the world collecting us like artifacts. If they manage to find some Native who has escaped all the crap and behaves like their ancestors, they expect the rest of us to be the same. The reality that some of us are rotters is too much for them.

"Don't ask me, I don't know who your mother was." Pretty low. He sat bolt upright in his chair and then waved me out the door. We were never close. Until then, he treated me in the same distant and friendly way he treated everyone else. At times he had been disgustingly condescending, even arrogant. After that remark he got real cold. At night I looked out my window screwing my eyes into the sidewalk and cudgelled myself for saying anything about his mother.

I could hear the rich laughter of Tony and his family next door. Probably Frankie was there cutting up the rug and laying out the laughs. I missed them.

I knocked. They didn't answer. I wondered why my feet just didn't walk in as usual. Shit. I must have stood for a couple of minutes arguing with myself. For the first time in my life it didn't feel right to just walk in on Tony. I made up my mind to go home and then the door swung.

"Jeez, sis. You scared me. I thought you must be cops or something." I backed up and he came out with me. We were both leaning on the porch and Tony started rolling a smoke. I handed him a tailor-made. His eyebrows went up.

"And do you have a savings account too?"

"With or without money in it," and he laughed.

"Well, now, you tell me."

"With." He turned to face the dark, pulling hard on his cigarette. My hand holding the extra tailor-made dropped uselessly to my side. That, too, was different. Nothing was usual anymore.

Tony's voice purred on gentle and slow. He told me they were dredging and filling False Creek again, making it smaller. Pretty soon we wouldn't be able to tell we had ever been here. I knew he was talking about me, us, changing our ways until we were just like them. I didn't say a word and he never got any closer to really telling me off than that. I left as soon as the story was over. Back in my room it dawned on me: he hadn't invited me inside. And the weeping began again.

The doctor worked out. We fell in love with her. She was soft spoken, thoughtful and enjoyed a good laugh when things looked their worst—just like us. She could hear every word you said and understand where they were coming from. She put up with no end of junk from some of her customers— patients she called them—and never laid their stuff on us. I got so caught up in the wonder of it all that autumn came and went without me thinking about the beauty of the colours of impending earth death or yearning for my mountains. Already, a slushy abysmal snow was trying to cover the sidewalks with some dignity. My mind was wandering around the endless days and nights of laughter that brightened the office down here. I had not thought of Tony or Frankie for a long time and the weeping got lost somewhere in the joy of our work.

I scraped all the tops of the mail boxes on the way to work, trying to get enough snow to toss in the boss' direction. He seemed like he wanted to break the ice between us and laugh again. This would do it. The door squeaked when I opened it, *doggone now he'll see me*. I slipped my hand with the snowball behind my back and peaked inside, softly giggling. There he was, holding the weeping doctor, a far-away angry look on his face. My insides started to shake. I tried not to think about anything. The snow was melting and my hand started to freeze. I tossed what hadn't melted outside while I urged the door shut as though reverent silence would fix things. I took a quick glance out so as not to hit anyone with my snowball. It had started to rain and I just closed my eyes. "Here it comes, here comes the night" was squeezing itself out on the radio.

"The clinic didn't get its funding and we are moving uptown." The words came out measured and flat.

"Why?"

"The city said they could not justify funding a racially segregated clinic."

"I meant the moving," bit words through clenched teeth. How could he possibly think I cared more about the clinic. It was her clinic, her white do-gooding conscience work. The office, that was ours. He squeezed her, she mumbled it was all right. I didn't look at her. He started in about how the Indians uptown were getting themselves into hot water fighting each other in the bars and the city. . .

"I don't give a shit about a horde of uptown Indians with

too much money and not enough sense not to kill each other. This. . . " I never finished. I bolted, slammed the door so hard the glass broke. I reeled on home thinking about winter, polka partners and this dirty town. Visions of assembly line women office workers still going about their jobs and white women doctors setting up shingles in other parts of town crowded between the sight of him moving despite his better judgement. My knees felt knobby, my legs too long, my hair lashed coarse at my face and the tawny brown on my skin became a stain, a stigma, like the street. Hope. Expectations. Great expectations I had never had. An office. A simple gawdamned office where we could breathe community into our souls was all we hoped for and it had been too much. I staggered down the street trying to hold onto little trivial bits of life that might help stabilize the rage. Old sidewalks are the only things in the world that age without getting dingy and dirty looking. The older they get, the whiter they look. Appropriate. And I am mad all over again. My feet play an old childhood game, "don't step on the crack or break your mother's back." Funny. I never thought about the significance of the ditty before. "Break your mother's back," and the first day the doctor came rolled into focus. . . "Don't ask me 'who is your mother?' "

All the games I ever played come back. Rough games, games which hurt the participants fill my memory. "Let's hide on Ruby," and little Ruby standing there in the middle of the sidewalk, silently weeping. Old grandma warning us, "Whatever you throw out will come back to haunt you." She never said it with any particular tone of voice—just kind of let it go matter-of-fact. The old mail box is turned over again. I set it right and lean on it and think about deserting Ruby like polka boy is deserting us.

Grandma, I wanted to say, you don't know the half of it. How was I suppose to know that the things I threw out would come back on the whole kit and caboodle of us. The liquor store to the left is calling me. I answer. Overproof rum, that'll shut up the nagging little woman whispering conscience material into my ear. Some old geezer wants a quarter. I am pissed enough to tell him to shut the fuck up. I look, open my mouth and then change my mind and move towards home.

Tony must have been watching me from his window on the old worn balcony of our project apartment home. I wasn't inside but a minute and a knock brought him through the door. He sits across from me just about where the slash of the curtain cuts a little sunlight onto his face. The rest of the room is semi-light. The trail of sunlight against his northern features makes him seem prettier than us from down here. No fat cheeks, just neatly chiselled high cheek bones, flesh stretching over them tight. His jaw is square and the hollow of his cheeks darker, sharpening his perfectly straight nose. He knows I am looking at him. He lets me despite his embarrassment, maybe sadness. I've known him nearly all my life and it was the first time I thought about how he looked.

"Can see the liquor store from here... looked like you were considering going in."

"Well, I never."

"Saw that too. But it don't stop me from wondering why. It's been a while for you hasn't it?"

"I guess I don't feel so young anymore."

A healthy "mnhmnh" and silence. In the still quiet I remembered Tony and Mose outside the tailor's before all this. I didn't go to the wedding, didn't even ask how it was. I was really scraping around inside my head trying to think about all the changes that had happened inside of me, trying to place snippets of new knowledge I'd gained and old habits I'd broken and make some sense of them. They whirled too fast. Memory after memory chasing each other in no particular order. It made me dizzy. The weeping is filling my gut, then Tony's voice tears up all the images.

"Saw Frankie today. Crazy guy. He ain't supposed to be driving. You know Frankie—talk a salesman into buying his own dictionary." My face wants to grin. "Cop stops him. He forgot to signal. Right away, Frankie jumps out of the car, lifts up his hood and pulls the plug out of the cap and tells me 'try her now.' " I'm smiling, nearly chuckling.

"Dumb cop says 'what seems to be the problem?' and Frankie says, 'I do not know officer, it just won't start.' He says it kind of condescendingly, but the cop, he don't notice. 'Let's have a look,' the cop says. Pretty soon, Frankie's in the car trying to start her while this cop is out there trying to fix what Frankie broke." The sight of Frankie and a serious young cop fussing over a half-dead Chevy in the middle of downtown traffic cracks me up. "Cop finally figures it out, all kinda proud, Frankie is no end to thanks, even puts the hood down. They say their howdy dos and off we go."

"Cops can be extraordinarily stupid."

"Now, now," Tony says, "You know they hire only the smartest morons."

"Now you going to tell me what the problem is? I didn't come here to entertain you for nothing you know." He is serious. It dawns on me that Tony hasn't been serious since he was a kid. Was it seventh grade? Yeah, in seventh grade Tony walked out the doors of that school and never went back. Why the hell did he leave? His question is still hanging on his face. I don't think I can answer him. Every time I try to think about that place too many thoughts get all crowded up together and none of them ever sits still long enough for me to figure anything.

"You really liked the place didn't you?" I nod. "Yeah, that boss of yours, pretty smart guy. Just breezed into town from Harvard or Yale or whatever university he come from, set it up and now he's breezing out again." He waits for this to sink in. "Come on outside, want to show you something." On the balcony he lights a smoke and leans into his own conversation. "See down there, Stace, just over there by the water. One time ol' Marta tells me, the shore come forward on the inlet—maybe a quarter mile or more. These people filled it up and put a sugar refinery on it. Yeah. Sugar is sweet, but you eat too much, you want more and pretty soon you're like Joey, forty and crippled with arthritis. You know what I mean Stace. One day water, next day sugar, next day pain."

"Shuddup." I lean against the wall. He tosses his cigarette over the balcony, tips his imaginary hat and strolls off. My bleary mind begins working away trying to get a hold of the significance of the story. It repeats it as though to memorize it so I can run it by me one more time on some other occasion when all my parts are working. The sun is sinking under a pall of dirty blue-grey haze. What was it? One day sweet, next day water. No. Shit. I lost it. The phone rings. Shit.

"Are you all right?" It's him. I consider slapping the phone on the table and then hanging up. The image makes me smile. Childish.

"Yeah. Shouldn't I be?" Someone should have kicked my butt a long time ago for letting the acid leak into my mouth and burn holes in my speech like that.

"You didn't look so good this morning." He is purring. That voice I recognize. Bastard, I think. I can see him leaning back on his chair, teeth flashing and voice curling up out of his lips confident and self-assured. He doesn't remember that I have seen him have seductive conversations with almost every other woman he talked to over that old black phone. He just can't help it; his sympathy begins and ends as a sultry invite. My tongue freezes. I stop helping him with the conversation.

"Look I would like to talk to you about this. I did what I could. Maybe not enough, but I ran out of words. The boys at head office... " Uncomfortable for him, these pauses—he can't handle dead air space. He fills it up with more bullshit. Then, "Can we meet and talk? There are some things you could help with." I see clearly for just a moment. That look he gave me when the doctor came. I could feel his look through the phone. Get the lead street girl on your side and the rest will follow. I could help him bring the downtown folks uptown.

"I can't haul furniture." My voice is as dead as I can make it. He doesn't notice. Maybe he can't hear. I laugh to myself. The bugger just can't stand losing. One last kick at the street. Pluck the rose left behind by tragedy. I want to play him. Hurt him, the way he hurt us. *Don't be a fool, guys like him got little tin badges and water pumps for hearts. They aren't made of flesh and blood.*

I can hear the tail end of his last line, "I didn't mean that." It sounds like a salesman who thinks he has his foot in the door. A wispy goodbye I was sure he didn't hear and I gently put back the phone. Without bothering to turn out the lights I slept. Slept the sleep of the dead. Dreamless. Lifeless sleep. I didn't ever want to wake. Sunshine played softly with the colours of my dusty lamps. The radio is playing old tunes. It must be noon. "You are my sunshine" cranks out tinny and ridiculous. I have heard that tune till I could just puke. Whoever she was, she did not live here, did not harbour futile dreams of dingy offices, and she never had to wrap up in a blanket in the dark without any hydro. She didn't know how it feels to crack cornball jokes about no hydro as though it was the best damned bit of fun you had had in a long time.

Hydro. Today's the last day.

I walk downtown. The office is just a deserted hole now. A dead office looks smaller, more confining than one alive with busy people. Memories of the people float about, wafting to the corners of my mind. I look away and stare hard in the direction of the hydro office. The sound of the street, the roar of cars grow louder. The murmur of hundreds of voices drowns the voices of my memory. I'm walking, not staggering. I can't resist peeking in at the 4-Star. Jimmy is still there. He is drumming the counter. Bored. One lone old white man sits in front of him eating his soup. Jimmy doesn't bother looking at him at all. "Nobody I know," and I laugh at the remark he always whispered to me whenever a white man entered. I decide to stop by on my way back.

I pass through uptown Granville on the way to the hydro

office. There they all are, a new crew, fixing up the building and in the middle of the crowd is my smiling polka boy. He sees me, lets his lips form a smile just like nothing happened. One day water, next day sugar, next day pain. Must have been the Pepsodent smile that reminded me, and I smile too. My eyes face his, but the whole of me is not looking at him anymore. The light changes and I turn, one last wave and cross. Everything after that is mechanical and unmemorable. I pay the hydro bill, experience rudeness from some prissy white girl and tell her that I understand. She works in an office. She looks as confused as polka boy when I leave.

Charlie

Charlie was a quiet boy. This was not unusual. His silence was interpreted by the priests and catholic lay teachers as stoic reserve—a quality inherited from his pagan ancestors. It was regarded in the same way the religious viewed the children's tearless response to punishment: a quaint combination of primitive courage and lack of emotion. All the children were like this and so Charlie could not be otherwise.

Had the intuitive sense of the priesthood been sharper they might have noticed the bitter look lurking in the shadows of the children's bland faces. The priests were not deliberately insensitive. All of their schooling had taught them that even the most heathen savage was born in the image of their own sweet lord. Thus, they held to the firm conviction that the sons and daughters of the people they were convinced were God's lowliest children were eternally good. Blinded by their own teaching they could not possibly be called upon to detect ill in the warm broad faces of their little charges.

Charlie did not do much schoolwork. He daydreamed. Much standing in the corner, repeated thrashings and the like had convinced him that staring out the window at the trees beyond the schoolyard was not the way to escape the sterile monotony of school. While the window afforded him the luxury of sighting a deer or watching the machinations of a bluejay trying to win the heart of his lady-bird fair, the thrashing he knew could be counted on for committing the crime of daydreaming was not worth the reward. So, like the other children, he would stare hard at his work, the same practiced look of bewilderment used by his peers on his face, while his thoughts danced around the forest close to home—far away from the arithmetic sums he was sure had nothing to do with him.

He learned to listen for the questions put to him by the brother over the happy daydream. He was not expected to know the answer; repeating the question sufficed. Knowing the question meant that, like the others, he was slow to learn but very attentive. No punishment was meted out for thick-headedness.

"What is three multiplied by five, Charlie?" The brother's brisk, clipped English accent echoed hollowly in the silence.

Charlie's eyes fixed on the empty page. His thoughts followed the manoeuvres of a snowshoe hare scampering ahead of himself and his half-wild dog. The first snow had fallen. It was that time of year. The question reached out to him over the shrieks of joy and the excited yelping of his dog, but it did not completely pluck him from the scene of his snow-capped, wooded homeland.

"Three... times... five?" muttered Charlie, the sounds coming out as though his voice were filled with air. A tense look from the brother. A quizzically dull look on Charlie's face. All the children stared harder at their pages—blank from want of work. He was still staring at the teacher but his mind was already following the rabbit. Did the brother's shoulders heave a sigh of disappointment?

"Thomas," the boredom of the teacher's voice thinly disguised.

"Fifteen," clearly and with volume. Poor Thomas, he always listened.

The bell rang. The class dutifully waited for dismissal. The brother sighed. The sound of scholarly confidence carefully practiced by all pedagogues left his voice at each bell. Exasperation permeated his dismissal command. It was the only emotion he allowed himself to express.

As he stood by the doorway watching the bowed heads slink by, his thoughts wandered about somewhat. *Such is my lot, to teach a flock of numbskulls. . . Ah, had I only finished and gotten a degree. Then, I could teach in a real school with eager students.* Each day his thoughts read thus and every time he laid out plans to return to university, but he never carried them out. At home every night a waiting bottle of Seagram's drowned out his self-pity and steadied him for the morrow.

* * *

Charlie was bothered at meal times. The food was plain and monotonously familiar: beef stew on Monday, chicken stew on Tuesday—the days with their matching meal plan never varied. Unvarying menus did not bother Charlie though. Nor was it the plain taste of domestic meat as opposed to the sharp taste of wild meat that bothered him. He was bothered by something unidentifiable, tangible but invisible. He couldn't figure it out and that, too, bothered him.

From the line-up, he carried his plate to the section of the eating hall reserved for sixth grade boys. He looked up to watch the teenaged boys exchanging flirtatious glances with the young girls in a line opposite them. In the segregated classes of the school, boys and girls weren't permitted to mingle with, talk to, or touch one another. They sat in the same eating hall, but ate on separate sides. Charlie bored quickly of watching the frustrated efforts of youth struggling to reach each other through the invisible walls of rigid moral discipline erected by the priesthood.

His eyes began wandering about the eating room of his own home. The pot of stew was on the stove. It always had something warm and satisfying to the taste in it. He scarcely acknowledged its existence before he came to residential school. Now he saw it each day at meal time.

At home no one served you or stopped you from ladling out some of the pot's precious contents. Here at school, they lined you up to eat. Each boy at each age level got exactly the same portion. A second plate was out of the question. He felt ashamed to eat.

A stiff-backed white man appeared in the room and the low murmuring of voices stopped.

"EAT EVER-Y-THING ON YOUR PLATE!" he bellowed, clicking out the last *t* on the word plate. His entrance never varied. He said the same thing every day, careful to enunciate each word perfectly and loudly, in the manner he was sure best befitted the station of principal of a school. He marched up and down the aisles between tables in a precise pattern that was designed to impress on the boys that he was, indeed, the principal of the school. Finished with the last aisle, he marched stiff-legged out the door.

The boys were more than impressed. They were terrified. They likened the stiff-legged walk to the walk of an angry wolf. They had come to believe that whites were not quite human, so often did they walk in this wolf-like way. They knew the man who had just pranced about the eating hall to be the principal, not by the superiority of his intellect as compared to the other instructors, but by virtue of his having the stiffest walk and, hence, the fiercest temperament of the pack.

Night came and Charlie prepared for the best part of his incarceration. Between prayers and lights out, the children were left alone for fifteen minutes. Quickly into pyjamas and to the window.

The moon and the stars spread a thin blue light over the whitening ground below. Crystal flake after crystal flake draped the earth in a frock of glittering snow. As always, a tightness arose in his small boy-chest. He swallowed hard.

"LIGHTS OUT!"

Darkness swallowed the room and his little body leapt for the bunk with a willingness that always amazed him. He did not sleep right away.

"Hay, Chimmy, you got your clothes on?"

"Yeh."

"Ah-got the rope."

"Keh."

Runaway talk! Charlie hurriedly grabbed some clothes from the cupboard beneath the top of the night-table he shared with another boy.

"Ah'm comin' too," he hissed, struggling to snap up his jeans and shirt.

"Hurry, we're not waitin'."

He rushed breathless to the closet and grabbed a jacket. The older boys had already tied the rope to the metal latticing that closed the window. Each boy squeezed through the square created by one missing strip of metal lattice, and, hanging on to the rope, swung out from the window, then dropped to the ground below.

Safe in the bosom of the forest, after a tense but joyous run across the yard, the boys let go the cramped spirit that the priesthood so painstakingly tried to destroy in them. They whooped, they hollered, bayed at the moon and romped about chucking snow in loose, small balls at each other.

Jimmy cautioned them that that was enough. The faster they moved the greater the head start. They had to get through the forest to the railroad tracks by night cover.

The trek was uneventful. The older boys had run away before and knew exactly where they were going and how to get there. Stars and a full moon reflected against white snow provided them with enough light to pick their way along. As time wore by, the excited walk became dull plodding. They reached the tracks of the railroad sometime near daylight. All were serious now. They cast furtive glances up and down the track. The shelter of darkness was gone. Discovery became real in the bright light of day. Surely the priest had sent the police in search of them by now.

The boys trod light-footed and quickly along the track-line, fear spurring them on. A thin wisp of smoke curling upward from the creaking pines on their right brought the boys to a halt.

"It's mah uncle's house," Jimmy purred with content-ment. The empty forest carries sound a long way in winter, so the boys spoke in whispers. It never occurred to the other boys to ask Jimmy what his uncle's reaction to their visit would be. They assumed it would be the same as their own folks' response.

A short trek through the woods brought them to the cabin's door. Uncle and aunt were already there to greet them. They were now used to the frequent runaway boys that always stopped for a day or two, then not knowing how to get home, trudged the nine and some miles back to school. The holiday, uncle mused to aunt, would do them no harm. Besides which, they enjoyed the company of happy children.

A good meal... a day's play... nightfall... heavenly sleep in this cabin full of the same sweet smells of his own cabin brought sentimental dreams to Charlie.

Charlie's dreams followed the familiar lines of his home. In the centre stood his mama quietly stirring the stew. Above her head, hanging from the rafters, were strips of dried meat. Hundreds of them, dangling in mute testimony to his father's skill as hunter and provider. A little ways from the stove hung mama's cooking tools. Shelving and boxes made of wood housed such food stuffs as flour, sugar, oatmeal, salt and the like. All here was hewn from the forest's bounty by Charlie's aging grandfather.

Crawling and toddling about were his younger brother and sister, unaware of Charlie's world or his dream of them. Completing the picture was his dad. He stood in the corner, one leg perched on a log stump used as a kindling split. He had a smoke in his hand.

No one but his wife knew how his thoughts ran. How he wondered with a gnawing tightness why it was he had to send his little ones, one after the other, far away to school.

Daily, he heard of young ones who had been to school and not returned. More often, he would come across the boys who recently finished school, hanging about the centre of the village, unwilling and poorly equipped to take care of themselves. Without hunting or trapping skills, the boys wasted away, living from hand-to-mouth, a burden on their aging parents. One by one they drifted away, driven by the shame of their uselessness.

It was not that they could not learn to hunt or trap. But it takes years of boyhood to grow accustomed to the ways of the forest, to overcome the lonely and neurotic fear it can sometimes create in a man. A boy who suddenly becomes a man does not want to learn what he is already supposed to know well. No man wants to admit his personal fear of his home.

The pull of years of priestly schooling towards the modern cities of a Canada that hardly touched their wilderness village grew stronger. For a while, family and city pulled with equal strength, gripping the youth in a listless state of paralysis. For some, the city won out and they drifted away. Charlie's father worried about the fate of his young ones.

His private agony was his own lack of resistance. He sent his son to school. It was the law. A law that he neither understood nor agreed to, but he sent them. His willingness to reduce his son to a useless waster stunned him. He confided none of his self-disgust to his wife. It made him surly but he said nothing.

In his dream, Charlie did not know his father's thoughts. He saw his father standing, leg-on-log, as he usually stood while he awaited breakfast, and he awoke contented.

Jimmy's uncle had given up wondering about the things that plagued Charlie's father. His children had grown up and left, never to return. He did not even know if there were grandchildren.

He lived his life without reflection now. Jimmy was the eldest son of his youngest brother. It was enough for his life's labours that this boy called him grandfather out of respect for the man's age.

"I'm going to check the short lines," he said, biting into his bannock and not looking at the boys.

"Can we help?" The older boys looked at their plates,

studiously masking their anxiety.

"Sure." Staring at them carefully, he added, "but the small one must stay." The old man was unwilling to risk taking the coatless boy with him.

Charlie followed them to the edge of the woods. He knew that no amount of pleading would change the old man's mind and crying would only bring him shame. He watched them leave and determined to go home where his own grandfather would take him to check his short lines.

The old aunt tried to get him to stay. She promised him a fine time. It was a wasted effort. He wanted the comfort and dignity of his own cabin, not a fine time.

Charlie knew the way home. It had not taken him long to travel the distance from the tracks near his home to the school. He had marked the trail in the way that so many of his ancestors might have: a rocky crag here, a distorted, lone pine there. He gave no thought to the fact that the eight-hour trip had been made by rail and not on foot.

The creaking pines, straining under the heavy snowfall of the night before, brought Charlie the peace of mind that school had denied him. A snow-bird feeding through the snow curled Charlie's mouth into a delighted smile. A rabbit scampered across the tracks and disappeared into the forest. He had half a mind to chase it.

"Naw, better just go home." His voice seemed to come from deep within him, spreading itself out in a wide half-circle and meeting the broad expanse of hill and wood only to be swallowed by nature's huge majesty somewhere beyond his eyes. The thinness of his voice against the forest made him feel small.

The day wore by tediously slow. Charlie began to worry. He had not seen his first landmark.

"Am I going the right way?" What a terrible trick of fate to trek mile after mile only to arrive back at school. The terror of it made him want to cry.

Around the bend, he recognized a bare stone cliff. Assured, he ran a little. He coughed and slowed down again. He tired a little. He felt sleepy. He touched his bare hands. Numb.

"Frostbite," he whispered.

In his rush to leave the dormitory he had grabbed his fall jacket. The cold now pierced his chest. Breathing was difficult. His legs cried out for rest. Charlie fought the growing desire to sleep.

The biscuits aunt had given him were gone. Hunger beset him. He trudged on, squinting at the sprays of sunlight that cast a reddish hue on the snow-clad pines in final farewell to daylight.

Darkness folded itself over the land with a cruel swiftness. It fell upon the landscape, swallowing Charlie and the thread of track connecting civilization to nature's vastness, closing with maddening speed the last wisps of light from Charlie's eyes.

Stars, one by one, woke from their dreamy sleep and filled the heavens. Charlie stumbled. He rose reluctantly. His legs wobbled forward a few more steps, then gave in to his defeated consciousness that surrendered to the sparkling whiteness that surrounded him. He rolled over and lay face up scanning the star-lit sky.

Logic forsook him. His heart beat slower. A smile nestled on his full purple lips. He opened his eyes. His body betrayed him. He felt warm again. Smiling he welcomed the Orion queen—not a star constellation but the great Wendigo—dressed in midnight blue, her dress alive with the glitter of a thousand stars. Arms outstretched, he greeted the lady that came to lift his spirit and close his eyes forever to sleep the gentle sleep of white death.

Lee on Spiritual Experience

California must be a magic place. Not only will it be the first state in the U.S. of A. in which the minorities combine to outnumber the white folks, but her colours dot our northern landscape. Pinks, pastel blues and rose-hued beiges colour new homes and apartments, diluting the powerful deep green of our mountains almost as though we needed some of the soft colours of California's desert to tone down the depth of our green.

Colours aren't the only things that have made their way across the forty-ninth parallel. In the mid-sixties the great flower child movement, or hippie movement, spilled onto the landscape of our hitherto apathetic social conscience. In the eighties new wave ideology began rushing north and we all became gripped by a deep need for spiritual enlightenment—real spirituality, the kind that motivates humans to behave more humanly. California catchwords colour our conversations: environmentally safe; politically correct; therapy; harmony and spirituality. (Now some nationalist is going to take exception to Americanizing what is seen as best about Canadians, but I heard all of these terms in San Francisco before I ever heard a Canadian utter them. Honest.)

The new wave movement for spiritual renaissance brings my folks back to the front of the bus, so to speak. Native North Americans are very spiritual—everyone knows that. Just before I go to read a new set of poems for Background Theatre, I watch David Suzuki on television; he is popularizing us again. "If we don't listen to Native people, who understand, have always understood the need to live in harmony with nature, who possess a spiritual bond with nature... " As he speaks, I wonder about myself. Almost every important

Native person I know has had some sort of powerful spiritual experience, except me. *Never mind, I tell myself, not having had a powerful spiritual experience has not dulled your vision, or your imagination.* I turn off the telly and sort through my work.

Let me say that I love a Six Nations Mohawk, married him and still continue to experience intense passion and wonderment after ten-plus years of living with him. Although our marriage has slipped into the comfort zone—you know, we get up every day, shit, shower and shave and go off to our different jobs (writing now being my job since publishers have started to market my words)—I can still be aroused to passion at thoughts of him. As the picture of Suzuki fades, I think of Dennis and decide to read my bent box poem about this lust/love. I further decide to pattern my reading after Pauline Johnson, Ka-Nata's first published Native poet and actress-comedienne extraordinaire.

The reading is in the whale room at Stanley Park. The park was Pauline's last place of comfort during the lonely days of her dying. It is all so fitting.

I always experience a deep sense of unreality, a feeling of unphysicality, before I read. Today, the absence of bodily consciousness is stronger than usual. There are three other women reading ahead of me. I know this, but my body doesn't seem to, and so it impatiently trots in the direction of the podium before my turn. The audience chuckles, the master of ceremonies corrects me and I return to my seat. My face is smiling sheepishly, but I am not quite in touch with myself so I don't feel my lips forming their embarrassed grin.

I watch the whales while the others read, and then drift off into my own world. "Properly rude," Chrystos would say. The whales are swimming about somewhat neurotically, as all people do when caged on a reservation too small for them to enjoy living. They are swimming in circles with Hyak, the man, on top and the two women underneath, in stairwell formation. Beautiful people of the sea. Poetry in motion, and I am lost in the sleekness of their skin, the elegance of their motion, and saddened by their imprisonment.

My turn. "I'm really glad to be here, tonight. Of course, every time I step out of that two thousand pound killing machine some man named a car, I am glad to be anywhere." The audience, mostly women my age, chuckles knowingly, and Hyak stands up in all his tumescent glory and chatters at me, seductively. "Yo, Hyak," I address him and carry on with my routine. "I turned thirty-nine last week, which was very important to me. It marks the last year of my youth, which is a good thing because I am the mother of four teenagers and I ought to grow up before them. This is the year I have been waiting for, the year in which nature does her duty by me and makes an adult of me.

"Maybe it has already worked, because I learned something about teenagers this year. Teenagehood is a crippling disease. I can tell because none of my children can walk anymore. Bus fares and car fares are eating up what little extra I have earned in royalties from my work. I raised every one of my children to be long distance runners, but as each reached teenagehood they ceased to be able to walk to the corner store. And it doesn't stop there.

"Teenagehood is also mind-crippling. Remember when they were five years old and they knew where everything was? You would come into the kitchen amid the orchestra of sound made by lids, pots and pans that the little ones were banging to create the kind of music only five-year-olds can appreciate. Nevermind, I told myself then, when they are older they will know where the pots and pans go. What a dream. Every time I go to cook, it's a major search to locate the tools of my trade. These children who have lived here, one of them for nineteen years and all of them for at least thirteen years, again and again put the pots and pans in a place different from where I've instructed them to.

"The other day my son who had just turned thirteen came into the kitchen with his fifteen-year-old brother—the one who decided last summer that 5'4" was an unseemly height for a man and set about adding seven or eight inches to his body. (I don't know whether it was seven or eight because my neck doesn't naturally strain sharply enough to properly assess his new height.) This mini-eruption has cost the fifteen-year-old in agility. He makes it into the chair all right, but his hand flies out and knocks over his glass of milk. 'Poor judgement,' he mumbles, not moving. I ask the thirteen-year-old to get a dishrag; I already know the older one doesn't speak this kind of English anymore...

" 'Ay?' very Canadian and very typically teenage.

" 'A dish-rag,' in that tone of voice only mothers use.

" 'Where?'

" 'Oh, try the stairwell.' Disappointingly, he does. I give up. He is afflicted: my last little genius has caught the disease of teenagehood and now I must wait another six years for him to recover. I join my other son in apathetically staring at the milk, plik-plik-pliking to the floor. I am in a marvelous state of self-rescue-catatonia therapy. My husband returns at the same time as my younger son; the one confused at not having found the dishrag on the stairwell and the other bewildered by my catatonic milk-spill watching.

"My husband, bless his heart, has become accustomed to this behaviour in the past few years and associates it (incorrectly) with my poetic disposition.

"Seriously, I love my children, but I look forward to the end of their adolescence."

Hyak is still jabbering at me, standing perfectly vertical, his huge manhood waving at me. *Hyak likes my poetry* I say innocently to myself and wonder what that thing waving at me is. *I must ask Dennis*, I note mentally. I read my love poem and Hyak looks as though the poem was written specifically for him.

Halfway through the poem, it dawns on me that these people are as captivated by my physical presence as they are by my words and voice. I feel, for the first time, absolutely lovely. I know I had no control over the face I possess, the contours of my cheekbones, the shape of my mouth and large eyes, but I can't stop feeling glad that these people think me lovely. I can't stop taking credit for it.

I rush off the platform to my husband's side and Hyak resumes his swim immediately after my read. Dennis touches my hand and says as he always does, "You did fine." I am not sure if it is his touch, his words or both, but this exchange always brings me back to the physical world.

"What was that thing waving in front of Hyak? It seemed to come from the middle of his body," I whisper.

"What do you think it was?" he says with the appropriate leer in his voice. A leer I had never heard him utter before. "He is a mammal, you know."

"No-o." Disbelief, shock and embarrassment all riddle my denial, but my insides confirm that *that* is exactly what it was. I think about spiritual experience, California colours, new wave and Native people. *And doesn't all that say something about your character, old girl?*

Too Much to Explain

She sat on the upper level of the lounge, her chair up against the wall. She didn't want anyone behind her tonight. The table she leaned on was small and dark. There weren't many people in the room; it was, after all, a Tuesday night in October. He was late. It twisted her insides that he didn't have the decency to be on time. *Just once, just once, you would think the bastard would be on time,* she thought with more venom than was called for. She tapped her cigarette rapidly at the ashtray and scolded herself for smoking so much. She closed her eyes hard to shut out the hum that plagued her ears. The sound of the tapping did little to cancel the hum and closing her eyes did less. She knew both gestures were futile, even absurd, but she made them anyway.

He entered the room with grace and dignity, took a quick look around the room from the doorway before he recognized her tucked up in a corner. *He's probably sizing up the women,* and the humming grew sharp. She resisted putting her hands over her ears. He nodded in her direction, smiled and strode over to the table.

From the door he had noted that she was thinner than when they first began seeing each other. Still, even thin she was lovelier than the other women he knew. He grinned at his own foolishness. It was not that she was so much lovelier but that he loved her; he liked the way his heart clouded his vision. She had been tense and inattentive lately. He wondered if this outing would suffer the same fate as the last two at Joe Kapp's. He tried to stop thinking about the harangues that had marred the last two occasions. Her smile quelled his momentary cynicism. He was embarrassed by his private recollection and his own suggestion that there might be a pattern developing here.

He stroked her hand lightly and pecked her cheek, then swung easily into the chair. She was nearly finished her margarita. His automatic display of affection did nothing for her. She feared that this exhibition was conducted more for everyone else's benefit—the way the lead wolf in a pack might covetously snuggle his females before younger hopefuls. She resented what might have been a perverse show of male possession. Her hand figetted slightly under his caress. A piece of her wanted to scream at him, but she knew that would not be rational. Rational people do not scream. The waiter came up just behind him and asked what they would like to order.

"Two margaritas," and he winked at her. She interpreted the wink and his sickening over-confidence as arrogance, mentally adding this to his list of crimes. *Gawd, what am I doing? Don't blow this,* and she felt colour come involuntarily to her cheeks. The floor floated towards her as the humiliation she felt filled her face. She argued with herself. *He's taking me for granted... Gawd, what a stupid catch-all phrase that explains nothing and everything that goes wrong between people. The waiter probably thinks I'm one of those ridiculous women lapel-roses that can't speak for myself.* She ignored the fact that she was still toying with a margarita she had ordered earlier.

The waiter rested his eyes on her momentarily, awaiting confirmation. She felt his gaze but ceded nothing. Seeing that she was not going to look up, he shrugged and left.

When she looked at the floor her lover was not sure whether she was bored or angry. Then he flushed. He had answered for her again. The realization brought a knot of anxiety to his gut. He sighed annoyance and looked off into space waiting for the barrel-load of condemnation that would assault his character, but it didn't come. He relaxed slightly, not bothering to reflect on his own internal need to eat up life's mundane and trivial decisions with his own decisiveness.

The pianist in the corner was plunking out a sad tune, "Moody River"; the sound was all the more melancholy in the absence of song and band. Just an old Black man, pecking at an even older piano. Pictures of her childhood home, the river and her solitary vigil next to it swam through her head. Her face wore a wistful smile when it turned to look at the piano player. Then her expression changed as she craned her neck to see.

"Dammit, the pole is blocking my view."

"Would you like to move?" he asked, trying to accommodate her. The question jarred her. A veil of darkness filmed her eyes.

"Why?"

Oh Christ, instant replay. When will I learn? Every time she invites me out like this, she gives me a hard time, but he didn't say that.

"Well, so you can see the piano player." He lit a cigarette. He rarely smoked and this little display of anxiety annoyed her.

"What do I want to look at some old man for?" She was rigid now, her words came out clipped into neat little pieces and were fed to him through tight lips. He sighed heavily, and even that she interpreted as male condescension in the face of a typical female airhead. The ringing hum in her ears gained volume as a steady stream of accusations whirled about insanely in her mind. Small bits of reason argued with the multitude of doubts until she finally regained her control.

He stared at the margarita in front of him and let his frustration drift around the dimly lit bar while his fingers played with the salty ice ring on the glass. Fatigue crept up on him like a faithless companion. He had been through this before with other women. He was beginning to think that this affair was going nowhere. Age and passion kept him rooted to his chair. He felt weighed down by an anchor of his own making.

"How did your day go?" She carefully laminated the

remark with layers of creamy sweetness. Surprised relief over-
took him. *He knows I'm pissed, why doesn't he say something. . .
stop that. . . Gawd,* and she recognized the voice that domi-
nated her thoughts. She fought to still the voice, to stop the
incessant humming. *Think of the river.* It swelled to a torrent
and gave way to a memory she had thought dead. The flood-
ing banks and the ranting of her mother returned to haunt her
and she wanted to faint.

"Another day of make work. If the new plans aren't ready
soon, I think I'll lose my mind." Her glazed look did not
escape him, despite her fawning attempt to disguise it. He
ignored it. *What the hell am I supposed to do?* he asked himself.
The question was in fact an old justification for doing nothing.

"Don't mock me." It slipped out too fast. *Oh God, there it
is, it's out, he'll guess.* Her fingers grabbed the napkin and tried
to ring the thought out of her mind by twisting the paper into
a white snake of anxiety. Far from surmising any hint of her
mental turmoil, he was confused by her response. Neither
confusion nor any of his other emotions had ever prompted
him to self-examination or indecision before, and he didn't
bother thinking about it now. The waiter rescued her with
another useless interruption.

It looked like they would be harassed all night by the
waiter's bored attentiveness. Her lover considered leaving but
didn't want to ask. *No sense inviting trouble,* he told himself,
and let the notion pass.

"I wasn't mocking you," he said with exaggerated
warmth. The pianist had stopped to change songs, so his
words echoed loudly across the emptiness despite his effort to
utter them softly. He reached for her hand. She feared that
non-compliance with his overture would call attention to her
near admission, but his hands inspired a feeling of revulsion
that she could not let go of and so she dropped her hands to
her lap. She concentrated on them guiltily.

"OK, what is it this time: my disgusting sexism, my

appalling arrogance or are you just generally dissatisfied with the meaninglessness of our relationship?" He laced the question with threat. His voice lied about the concern for his character that his question implied. The noise in her ears rose an octave. The pitch of it deafened her. It blocked out the reality of the bar. The roar of the river on top of the ringing in her ears distorted everything.

The table became a watery seductive maw, the glass a slender woman staggering and begging to be let go. The weaving woman-glass swayed frantically in the clutches of her own liquid indecision, its every movement an accusatory cry to her for decisiveness. She threw the glass at the table. The margarita bled the content of her memory across the table and it leaked onto the floor. She jumped up babbling about stress, weakly trying to submerge her behaviour in neurotic nonsense. He signalled the waiter, relieved that he had not seen her throw the glass, and was sorry that his remark had been so harsh.

She stood aside while the waiter finished mopping up the drink with his rag. Her body hung limp against the wall. She knew she couldn't keep this façade up much longer. She wanted the floor to swallow her. She prayed that the river of her maddened mind would drown her. Anger abated, he looked at her more seriously now than he could remember doing. Her thinness took on dimensions of anorexic vulnerability. Her strangeness seemed less excusable.

"Is school getting to you?" he asked. She clasped her hands together with too much vigour. That voice, that "nancy nursey" voice drove her to the edge. She struggled to collect herself. She fought to rest her nameless agitation on something plausible.

"Don't patronize me. Who do you think you are? You just sit there like you are the only person in the world who can handle life. You don't think I can deal with anything, do you?" The words jerked out too fast between clenched teeth. Her eyes narrowed to slits. She would have said more but the stupid waiter was back again like a phantom, cajoling them to have another drink.

"A double daisy for me," she hissed.

"Huh?" The rude bugger didn't have the sense to say "pardon me." She didn't answer. She turned to face the wall and tugged at her cheek with tensed fingers.

"Two double margaritas," her lover said politely. The waiter sensed the tension and left quickly. She wanted to start in on him again, but scenes of the river broke her concentration. Instead of the usual hazy images of the past, the pictures took on a dangerously lucid clarity. *Maybe if I just let it happen. . . maybe if I just lose myself in the lousy nightmare of it all instead of trying to stomp it out with rattling nonsense. . .*

He was near the breaking point. *I'm just a gawdamn nailpounder, not a fucking therapist. What the fuck do I know about her feminist anxieties,* and he closed his eyes. This was more than he could deal with. *Fuck yourself* was what he wanted to say, but he continued sitting there for reasons he could not adequately explain to himself.

The blood drained from her fingers and her hands shook from the loss. Weakly, she stood up and numbly walked to the bathroom. He paid the bill. When she returned they left.

The sound of the traffic failed to reach her and he had to hold her trembling body against him at the curb to prevent her from stepping out among the cars. He let her lead him into the blackness when the traffic cleared. The world was getting farther away from her. She needed to hear the water, it floated around in her head like a torrent of frustrated feminine rage, liquid unpredictability. They walked wordlessly forward and the hill rolled up behind their scurrying legs.

False Creek lurched into view at the bottom, a poorly lit facsimile of cultivated wild wood and trail. Over the hill of manicured lawn and untended brush the creek stretched out purple black against a neon skyline. No other lovers were out. The night was cool and the city's citizenry were already asleep in anticipation of the morrow's work.

They climbed down the man-made stone embankment. At the bottom, she sat with knees up, her shins folded in her thin, shivering arms. She hugged herself, waiting for the ringing to subside so the pictures she had long suppressed could return. She forced herself, in the comfort of the night's quiet affection, to watch it all.

He wrapped her in his jacket and waited helplessly. He had no idea what was going to happen but his sense of chivalry and his knowledge of the city would not allow him to desert her. He resigned himself to a night of cold anticipation.

From the river bank she saw her mother struggling with her husband, screaming at him to give her her papers. . . silly little bits of brown bags and napkins that she had scribbled on. He had caught her scribbling poems again. Her six-year-old body watched him through her woman's mind, and the clarity of the moving picture in her mind surprised her. At the end of her memory's eye, her mother disappeared over the roar of the river and her drunken father staggered uselessly after her, calling her name as though she were deserting him and not perishing under the hands of his drunken rage.

"They said I was crazy, a bonafide nutcase." Her chuckle came out a murmur. It was the kind of chuckle women let out when they suddenly discover that the mysteries surrounding unplugging a toilet are pathetically simple and wonderment is unwarranted. Her lover lived quite outside her range of subtle emotional variance and so thought the chuckle evidence of the truth of the findings of whoever "they" were, rather than recognizing it as the "I'll be" chortle of realization. He didn't want to hear it. *Christ, what am I supposed to do with this?* He didn't move or answer her aloud. There must be more, and he waited for it. He stared at the lights reflected against the water and thought about how they, too, made a crazy dance pattern against its smooth surface. He rested his face against her neck, trying to search his mind for some hope.

"I spent most of my childhood yo-yoing between lonely foster homes and a mental ward. . . Shit." She began to rock back and forth. Her memories rolled into the smooth lap of False Creek as the wall of fear and veil of confusion lifted. She couldn't leave the brutal trap her father had set for her. The little girl, traumatized by the scene, had jumped inside the same trap, running a marathon of imprisoning relationships because she had not wanted to remember. Now the trap sunk.

"The little girl just had no words." He couldn't accept that she was crazy, but this last remark wanted some point of reference to make it rational. If he accepted her insanity he would have to declare insane the hysteria of his mother, the violence of his sister and her breakdown, and his own mad-dened binges of the past. He would have to condemn them all because he just wasn't cut out for looking inside at the why of himself or anyone else. He resigned himself to a crazy destiny, half wishing that he had been born snugged up against the dis-tant mountains of his ancestors a half millenium earlier.

"You don't have a monopoly on craziness," he said dully. She laughed at his flat sense of self, at the hopelessly two-dimensional perception that he clung to, and she wondered if the man who defined neurosis wasn't just a little like her lover. Without feeling the least bit guilty about the unfairness of leaving him like this, she handed him his coat and left without saying goodbye.

He followed her up the hill and she left him there in a tangle of confused babbling while she climbed into a cab and drove out of his life. It was all too much to explain. How does one begin to unravel the accumulation of thousands of years of entrapment to a man bent on repairing the rents she occa-sional made in the machinery of the trap.

"I just don't feel desperate anymore," was all she could come up with. As the cab sped away she could hear him holler in self-defence, "You really are crazy."

Sojourner's Truth

From inside my box, an ugly thought occurs to me. I know what hell is—actually, I knew it all along, but in my haste to barrel along and live, I had not thought about it until just now. Hell just might be seeing all the ugly shit people put each other through from the clean and honest perspective of the spirit that no longer knows how to lie and twist the truth.

Can you imagine, there you are watching some maniac jerk his wife or kids around, pulling arms out of their rightful places in sockets and you walk on minding your own business, only this time you don't feel like just shuffling along and ignoring it. Your spirit cries out for humanity, but all you get to do is weep and remember that you didn't care when your soul was housed in living meat. You could have struck a blow at violence against women and children, but the little whisper from your living soul was drowned by the reality of all that flesh.

In its final resting pose your soul knows that all the maxims that guided your hypocrisy are just so much balderdash. "Spare the rod and spoil the child." "Don't let her get away with it." Whoever heard of such a ridiculous proposition! "Don't drop the apples, they bruise easily" is more like it. Pictures of all the lickings I laid on Emma and the kids file through my mind. In my newly dead state I try to rationalize one more time: if you don't subject the kid to a certain amount of brain rot, the kid is apt to object to even a minimum of authoritarian discipline. Hell is seeing the lie in all your excuses.

My thoughts come to an abrupt halt. I know that I am in the box and must get out. How convenient: the very moment you realize that you must get out, there you are outside, watching everyone from the most advantageous viewpoint. They are all gathered around the box. Those that talk are whispering as though they might interrupt the soul of me; others are in tears. The kids are playing. Why everyone gathers around the boxes housing the bodies of the dead is beyond me, though. The truth of me has long left the box.

The truth of me is a little unnerved by the realization that there are not as many living bodies gathered around my box as I expected. I face it, though. What the hell did I expect? I didn't do anything to inspire anyone to show up and grieve my departure, permanent though it is. (At least there aren't any Chinamen.)

Oh God, there are a hundred thousand Chinamen living in this city and I cannot count even one of them as a human being who will miss me. I weep. No tears, just the kind of pain of the inner self that goes with the action; the sort of hot, wracking emptiness, but without the tears to cool it off. There aren't any Indians or Blacks. *Oh God, there aren't even many white people here.* I lived for seventy years moving around in a sea of almost a million people and only fifty show up to bury my body and bid my spirit adieu.

"It's a crying shame, he wasn't that old." Thanks, Mike, but it really isn't a shame. Death is natural, but then we are inclined to add shame to all that is natural. The naked body and spirit is a deep source of shame to the mortal beings crawling about the earth. Life does look a little different from the vantage point of death.

A ripple of pleasure overtakes me as Emma speaks. "You know he didn't take care of himself." It is the worst she could come up with and still wear a mask of polite mourning. Hate jumps out at me and for a moment the essence of me is seared by it. A storm of hidden knowledge, secret pain, leaps at my soul, accusing, huge in its condemnation of my treatment of her as wife. I can see where it all comes from: the mind-bending brutality, the intimidation, the violence, the erasure of her soul—the screaming soul she denied. *Oh God, the living body of me scarred and twisted the very soul of Emma.*

In a corner, my brother and sister are secretly plotting for the spoils of my bodily being. Jerks. My spirit rolls back to my own plotting for the spoils of my parents before they were properly laid to rest. The twisting begins again, the terrible, unbearable heat of deceit in life burns my soul in death.

Oh God, I cry, *Don't do this to yourselves.* No one hears me. It is a little confusing being dead. You feel more alive than ever, except no one knows you are there. No soul present actually misses me, most particularly not Emma. She is relieved.

Shit. And mountains of it appear from nowhere. Shit loads tumbling down from above me. A wall of crap. *I don't believe this.* The spirit of me is swept up in this sheet of rank-smelling human feces. *What's going on here?* We hit the water together, the shit and the truth of me. The water is filthy without the help of the crap. Rushing along, spreading itself out, and running for the vast bankless river of salt, the crud holds my truth in a vice-grip of gut-wrenching stink. *What the hell is this all about?* The water ejects me at the exit of the river just next to an old man sitting on a park bench reading a newspaper.

I remember it now. Three million metric tonnes of untreated sewage dumped into the Fraser River, protested, of course, by a few crazies—college rejects, calling themselves eco-something or others. *Oh God. I wish I had been one of them.*

Hey, you oughta be reading that with a little more soul, old man. The polluting happened before I died so my words are wasted, but the truth is, it still goes on.

On the wings of a snow white dove, my truth sails across the vast expanse of weeping earth and choking fauna and my soul mutters helplessly to the wreckage below: *Jesus, I didn't know.*

"Oh yes, but you didn't seek." From out of the blue, he appears on the tip of the dove's other wing, looking just as normal as can be. He can't be normal, though—he must be just as dead as me. The dove dips and drops us both in a mountainous wasteland—earth brutalized by a flurry of murderous chainsaws that massacred her treasured children. Not satisfied, man consigned the weak, the unusable seedlings and brush to a widow's pyre.

Didn't seek? I repeat dumbly.

"Yes, you know, seek and ye shall find," and he fades away.

WAIT.

No presence, just a soft chuckle and a clean voice: "You silly fellow, you cannot command another man's soul here."

Oh Lord.

"That's another thing, that whole business of lords has no roots in heavenly reality." At first I think he is kidding. But after I listen to it, I realize the whole notion of lords in heaven is ridiculous. It could not have been contrived by ethereal souls.

From inside the stone walls of Parliament, the House of Lords drivels nonsense while their lying souls convince their mouths that the bullshit they are peddling is true. I can't believe that I ever had faith in these fools. It's embarrassing. "Apartheid is not a question for us to address," some wigged lord with South African investments is saying. *I'll bet not. After all, you're the white guys.* I would laugh, but the truth stops me and there in the kitchen of my own neighbourhood is Mike, being disgusted by all the uppity Blacks "who had a lotta nerve shooting us," and the body of me is agreeing. The blood of Soweto runs thick in the kitchen. The screaming pain of children being shot fills me. It muffles the stupid words uttered by pompous arrogance, and soils forever my truth.

A child, heartsick and ashamed, appears in the school yard with my grandson, who leads the others in cruel taunts against the solitary child.

Oh don't. Jesus don't.

"I never did. I always maintained that all children are a

great offering to life." There he is again and the truth of his African heritage is written on his soul.

Actually, I was talking to my grandson.

"His name is not Jesus," and he disappears.

Is this all there is? Endless pictures of the whole suffering world? The wind carries my longings to the mouth of a poet whose words are secretly laughed at. *Oh God,* and a vast sense of nothingness sweeps over me. The nothingness is unmoving, cloying in its inertia. It suspends my soul in a terrifying void. It ends like it began, suddenly and of its own will. Nothingness is scary, but still it offers temporary relief from the tearless weeping. Since I came to this God-forsaken place, I have laughed but once.

In the meadow where the void jerks to a halt, children are playing, chasing illusive butterflies. Peace rests within me. Laughter delights their little bodies, captures the heart of the grasses, and the trees chatter, echoing the sensuous happiness of childhood. The sun whispers gently and its light plays about on the skin of earth's young. Grass, trees and little children are swollen with peace and joy. It is the first moment of rest for my soul.

"Growth is joyous. The knife that inhibits growth is the sword of death," the grasses breathe in blessed refrain.

The children disappear and a plane carrying defoliants flies overhead spraying the meadow below in preparation for clear-cutting the forest at the edge of the meadow. The horror of the whir from the airplane's engine slaps the peace from my soul.

Jesus, when does it all end?

"Be clear. When does what all end?" (*Jesus, I am getting tired of this guy. Every rhetorical or philosophical remark prefaced by his name calls him forth.*)

"You won't be so tired when your novitiate is over. I don't have to answer forever, you know." I did not know that there are no private thoughts in heaven. Jesus smiles.

Well, the butchery?

"Ah," and he leaves. The earth sighs to the sun, "It ends when the body of people stop hiding from the truth of the spirit." It seems too simple.

"It is simple. Why are you, of all people, doubting that?" she asks. And suddenly, I need the comfort of Emma's long suffering presence...

*   *   *

"Hallo-oo, how ahre you?" and the lilt in Mike's voice veils his discomfort at seeing Emma again. He doesn't want to know how Emma is. His deception is an ugly sight. Deception has got to be hell's inner face. A deluge of scenes of deception bombards my truth: verbal garbage, physical garbage and most criminal of all, food garbage—all deceptively rationalized as respectable by the bodies of humanity that race across my view. The soul of people takes the shape of their deception, and the eyes of my essence ache with the unbearability of the sight.

Jesus. What is going on?

"Well, this is heaven and here you are, dead, looking at life through the honest eyes of your soul."

Well, if this is heaven, what is hell?

"You already know the answer to that one. Perhaps you want to know more about how it all works. You see, heaven is simply the sky. At the point of mortal departure, your spirit gets to walk the wing tips of the wind witnessing the reality of your life. The soul is not blind, however. In death the truth is not dressed in the deceptive clothes of mortal flesh. The soul is incapable of rationalization."

You mean I have to watch over and over, everything I have just seen?

"That is about it, but for a minor exception."

What do you get to see—the same thing?

And he laughs. The sound comes from deep within the earth, rich and resonant. It spreads out thick and joyous. The winds catch the laughter and layer the seas and grasses with it. Embarrassed, I try digging around inside for guilt to hide my shame. Only shame blossoms, relentless in its flowering. I yearn for the agony of guilt to absolve me. I fall over in a foolish, prostrate position of remorse, but guilt does not come.

Oh Jesus, can't I even enjoy the comfort of guilt?

"Oh no. Heaven is not like that. Here, there is but pleasure and pain. You see, if pain were experienced with the absolving comfort of guilt, it would be impure. Guilt is an intellectual contrivance that reduces the pain the spirit needs to experience if it is to alter the actions of the body. In that sense, guilt is the ultimate deception—hell. The spirit resides in heaven; it knows not hell."

Holy mother of Jesus. I can't go through this for all eternity.

"Yes you can. People do it all the time." She said it without sympathy—just a matter of fact, eternal reality.

"Hello mom," Jesus purrs.

"Jesus, how nice for our paths to cross."

Christ, this is insane. I balk at the bizarre meeting between mother and son, two thousand years dead. In my mortal life the idea of Mary as Jesus' mother ended with his birth.

"You called?" Jesus interrupts my thoughts.

I meant God, really.

His voice swells with magnificent urgency: "Man in his opportunist desire to ease life and deceive himself that the torment of others is no concern of his distorts the natural world of the spirit. Man creates a vision of heaven and hell for himself that he might justify his selfishness and appease his conscience while outraging human and natural life. God, good, all began as the 'great offering' of one's life to the world. But now, it is a catch-all word for every kind of desperate anguish living mortals wish to hide from. The offering is disempowered, destroyed and its meaning lost to humanity by the distortion of godliness. God has become the mantle for the greatest human atrocity—war."

Horseshit, I snap, and it begins again, the crap, the children, the hunger of humanity.

Oh Jesus. I want to go back to my box and rest.

"You can't. It has been buried. Heaven is the sky and you cannot return to the earth. How long did you think eternity was?" Jesus leaves and the terror of having to walk the winds witnessing my life's trials without the comfort of his company follows his departure. The memory of my mortal life, cold nights warmed by Emma's yielding flesh, fill me with desire. *Emma, help me.* Below my shameless begging stands Emma, staring hard at the window of her quiet living room. She hears nor sees a thing. She is busy making a decision.

"He seems like a nice fellow. Not like the last," she whispers silently to herself, not even according me my name or the title of husband. "Ah courtship, if only love could grow from the sweet seed of courtship to the lovely flower marriage was intended to be." The inside of her new love lays itself bare to me. While the man's body anxiously occupies my chair and waits for her reply, his damaged soul shouts his truth at mine. I try to warn her but know she hears not a word. Alone at fifty-six, afraid, desperate for affection, Emma says "yes."

In the beginning he is sweet, as though he has not fully awakened to the realization that the courtship is over. For a while there is laughter in Emma's little house. But, as men are wont to do from time to time, he screws up at work. The boss gives him "what for" and he comes home, full to the brim with another man's anger and his own humiliation.

Like a replay of my own mortality, the beer follows, then drunken, impotent raging about the boss, and wild, unreasonable demands on Emma. She is slow to move on his drunken commands. (Sabotage, I had surmised as a living person, and quite correctly. What woman jumps happily to a drunken husband's command?)

Then the fists fly. The thud of human meat battered by the hammer that can be a man's hand. The tears, the screams, the agony of his perverse triumph over the lively body that he alone has reduced to limp life. And my wasted soul stretches itself over her body in a futile effort to protect my Emma from this other man's fists.

Inside the body of Emma a black emotion rises and spirals to the centre of her being. The soul of me catches in the madness of her emotion, captivated by her bleakly intense struggle to convert her outrage to despair. A crazy cacophony of raw passion carries me to that magical place where all feelings begin. A single crystal teardrop, alone in a fit of rage, rests peacefully. In shocked disbelief, my truth stares at the perfect droplet.

Jesus...

"But it is beautiful, isn't it?" His voice brings momentary relief from the desperation that lingers in the clarity of the tear.

Is this all there is left, just one tear, one tear to account for her entire life?

"Imagine, if you will, that she can hear the mutterings of her innermost self and rise up. Imagine the great flood that this little tear could become in the tide of her resistance. Bear witness, my friend."

Jesus fades and compassion rises in the soul of me. My soul envelopes the tear. I plead for its life, praying for it to swell and to multiply. Softly murmuring, I cajole the tear to grow. *Not twice, Emma. I am dead. Surely you must know that I should never have lived thus, comfortable with your suffering. Emma, hear the words whispered to thee by thy self, thy perfect self. Abide by thy perfect right to be.*

I stretch my truth throughout her body, grow small around the tear, my soul rhythmically undulating with my fervent desire for her salvation. My love reaches its purest moment. Spent, my passion drapes itself in a perfect circle around the lonely tear. I feel her body rise. I hear the resounding "no" from every cell of her flesh. In my death watch, there is great rejoicing. The knife in her hand drives through the sleeping man's heart. The blood mesmerizes her and then the wall of tears drives me outside herself.

But more my spirit knows. Police and courts are next. Emma sits in wordless teary repose, my own madness her defence. "Not twice." The very words of my soul she repeats to her counsellor. From my sky perch I am compelled to watch. Jesus came first among the throng that gather. Curious, I ask why his presence.

"This is the very thing to which I am called, the judging of the meek and courageous by the lords of violence."

Nine Black boys gather next to us, giggling and shuffling and watching by turns.

Who are they?

"The Scottsborough boys. You must remember them."

How could I forget. The boys hung for a rape they were much too innocent to commit. The madness of racism runs sour and acrid in my soul. I, coward that I was, sanctioned the dirty deed. Sympathy, simpering and jelly soft, obscures my outrage.

It must have been terrible for them to come here.

"Not at all. They have enjoyed themselves immensely since being freed from the prison of racial violence. Why, they have participated in every glorious riot, in every move-ment of Black resistance from Birmingham in 1948 to Soweto, just a short time ago. They have had their vengeance."

Is there then only freedom in death?

"Quite the contrary. When the slave is no longer a slave, what you have left is an ex-master. If the master insists on protecting his position with weapons, the slaves will have to covet the gun."

The congregation includes the strangest people.

Who is the funny-looking little fellow who speaks a strange language?

"Why that's Vladimir Ilyich Ulyanov, you probably know him as Lenin."

But he is an atheist.

"Heaven is the one place that does not discriminate."

The congregation swells its ranks with the champions of

the meek and poor: those who so loved the world that they sacrificed their selves that justice to earth and people might prevail. Marx, Fred Hampton, Jackson, Krupskya, Gwarth-Es-La and his standard bearer. . .

These people are all rebels.

"Yes, they are all in their own way like myself."

I am no rebel.

"Ah, but you unlocked the door to Emma's rebellion."

The court case drags on in its usual ceremony of arrogant rigidity and stupid exactitude of language without sentiment. My life with her is dragged forward couched carefully in legal mumbo-jumbo. Her character is attested to by women who assure the world that Emma was a kind and devoted wife to a brutal first husband. Even our children testify that they and their mother had been abused. Emma rises to her own defence. She refuses to deny that her hand held the knife that stabbed her second husband, but she confesses no guilt.

"I am a Christian woman. This is supposed to be a Christian country. Jesus himself forbade the abuse of the meek, but he did not deny our sacred right to resist abuse. 'Where ye shall have no justice, ye shall have no peace.' The man that would batter his wife is less than a serpent. I was born three months ago; until that day, I wandered the world a slave. . . "

"Oh, ain't she a woman?. . . Ain't she a woman?" and the tall reedy body of an old Black woman waltzes and sways to the music of her own words.

Who are you?

"Why, I'm Sojourner Truth. An' Emma an' me was born on the same day. I was delivered from slavery at fifty-six years ol' and so was she."

"I should have killed that first brute," Emma says, "but he died on me. And this lawyer sitting here doesn't know what he is about. Didn't know what I was doing? No one who feels the plunge of a blade through the human heart can ever testify that they did not know what they were doing. I knew I stabbed him. I knew it would send him to his maker. But I am guilty of no crime. I did not kill a man; I stabbed a snake."

The judge looks aghast. She feels her own emotion rising, contemplates quitting herself of the case, but a voice whispers from within that the jury, not she, would be pronouncing the verdict on Emma. She remains riveted to her throne. She counsels the jury that she must resolve some legal questions before they can retire to decide Emma's fate, and she buys time for her own troubled soul.

In the week that follows, the congregation remains vigilant. There is a hubbub of discussion about the possibilities that lay ahead for woman and earth should Emma win. Joy hangs in the air, visible as Thoreau's lily. Even the old woman next me, grim-faced most of the time, chuckles now and then.

What is your name?

"Emily."

Carr, the artist?

"Hmph."

I am honoured, I pule.

"I would rather you be enjoyed."

The week draws to a close and the judge counsels the jury. "The defendant takes precedence over her own counsel. Indeed, according to Benjamin Franklin, Thomas Jefferson and the 'defender of the constitution', Daniel Webster, the founding fathers of this United States of America intended the values of this country to reflect those of the New Testament. The jury is to decide the fate of Emma in accordance with the book of Revelations and the word of Jesus. There is no doubt that Emma slew her second husband, but the law governing America and finally Emma, is the law of Christ."

The jury retires, armed with twelve New Testaments. And the heavenly congregation replies in blessed song:

> Praise her soul, she saw the light
> The truth of this sojourner,
> has been seen at last.
> Praise her soul, she saw the light.

World War I

I wonder about memory sometimes. As a child I, along with a host of other children, listened to story after story without ever considering we would one day want, no, need to repeat these stories. I have repeated a number of such stories to my own children on long winter evenings during winter sleep, but until now I never wanted to write any of them down. Some I will never tell, but this one is curiously apropos to our times and it gnaws at me as though it wants to find its way to dead wood leaves. I never thought much about the accuracy of my memory. Fiction does not require it, but this one isn't fiction; it happened, even if it didn't. Right now I don't even trust my memory to tell you who the bearer of the tale was. I was busy stewing over this when it struck me that the gift I possess lies in coming to grips with the essence of a story and combining this essence with my own specific imagination.

In my memory, no two people ever told the same story in exactly the same way. The bearer of the tale embellished the thread of the story with their own fabric. It would be sad should this written version come to represent the last word in the story; hence, I caution you to read it and re-imagine it, tell it to yourself with your mind wide open and full of your own embellishments.

There is a rush upon us, a tidal wave of soul-searching of the past. All manner of youth are returning to the firesides of the elders in our community to gather yesterday's stories and commit them to memory. I don't feel this urge as deeply as I ought to. I return to no one to refresh my memory, perhaps because I am old enough to believe that, young as I am, I understand what I heard, and perhaps because I believe that the thread of it, not the precision of its retelling, is what is important.

For those with a penchant for verbatim accuracy, the story will offend. I don't apologize. For those who learned from the story *when you first heard it and let it guide your lives, the story will enthrall and inspire, and this I am keen on.*

* * *

Characters: Him, un-named animal, probably extinct
SHE, definitely extinct

Two eagles, an ailing old man and his long time mate, enjoy his last movements. No tears from her, just resignation. She watches him draw his last breath, noisy and full of objection to the termination of his life. His passing occurs amid a storm that rages across the bits of land left by rising water. Great bodies pool into lakes fed by a confusion of streams which meld with salt water of the seas. A tempest of liquid—swirling, bubbling and prohibiting the flourishing of new populations—had gone unnoticed by the old woman until her mate's life was over.

In the joy of their union, she had not thought about the shrinking of the landscape. With his death, her eyes opened to the creatures huddled together between the mass of moving lakes, streams and sea, birthing and perishing on the narrowing ridges before maturity reached them. She knew something momentous was about to happen.

The bird people were reduced to flying incessantly, sneaking up on the entrapped four-leggeds while they slept, in order to garner a few seeds and insects. Confined to ridges, the animal people grew sour, mean, bickering among themselves, unable to develop the character of their race in a balanced way. When hunger came upon them, and it did more and more often, they snarled, nipped and occasionally ate one another. Their sleep was incomplete as the sleep of the hungry is apt to be.

Suspicion, hunger's lover, distorted them, grew to paranoia; bickering became feuding and genocide threatened the people. Rain was anticipated with dread. It filled the lakes, over-ran the streams and halved the little existing ridgelands, decimating entire populations. Whole species came and went during the rains. Plant life perished and starvation, not the simple hunger that natters at the body between mealtimes but starvation of the sort which emaciates and destroys the body, swallowed one species after another. Eagle, her mate gone, took it upon herself to examine the world.

* * *

From a ridge, he watched the water swell. His ridge was shrinking, the water was swallowing the bit of earth under his feet. Great huge raindrops pelted his coat. Shivering, he peered over the landscape with panicked eyes bulging inside their fleshless sockets. He staggered towards the water, scanned the next ridge: maybe it would produce a drowned rat, a mole. Despite his fear, he leapt into the raging inferno.

Each pathetic stroke brought new panic to Him as the water, maddened by the rain, rose and fell, pulling at the living skeleton, thrashing at it as it struggled to reach the next ridge. A mouse, eyes blank with lifelessness, was tossed to Him in mid-stream. He swallowed it. Whole. Barely chewed its scrawny body. He gagged, the blood rushed to his head, dimmed his eyes, his stomach worked overtime trying to digest the thing. Water snuck inside his nose and stopped the need to gag while it threatened his lungs with asphyxiation.

Memories tormented Him, memories of his young eaten by himself, and of his mate, murdered in his bitter determination to survive. These memories stilled his legs. *What is the point, you have no mate, your survival is limited to this, your last swim.* The thought of the end of his species calmed Him. *No more scrounging, no more swimming for new shores, the end of eating newborn in vain attempts to survive.* His relief at coming to the end relaxed Him and his body gave up its desperate strokes, acquiescing to a melancholy dreamlike floating on the crest of the torrent of water.

From deep within the bowels of the earth a volcano erupted, driving the water straight up and fanning it out. The sea raged, churned, and bits of earth were cast to a special place. *Dream, old boy, dream of earth lush and green, of landscapes rich and relenting, dream through the whirl of sea and flying earth.* Stone, inert, cool stone driven from the sea fell layer upon layer onto the ridge in front of Him. Earth bits covered land and island mountain was created. Animals in their multitudes peopled this new place while he floated on the sea.

He was aware he was dreaming. He knew he dreamed this dream in one last attempt at eternity. Sleep, deep, dreamless and long, came upon Him and he all but succumbed to the ravages of the rain and sea. Eagle, in her wanderings, came upon Him. She thought of SHE. SHE, lonely, her life empty of the company of her own. Eagle whistled and Raven joined her. The thought of gifting SHE with one of her own appealed to Raven. (Raven is not always a trickster; sometimes she's downright kind.) She swooped down and plucked Him from the turbulent waters and tossed Him to the shores of their island mountain home. Eagle tracked SHE down and whispered of the presence of Him.

SHE's cool tongue caressed his cheek and cleaned his aching body. It woke Him up. SHE looked at Him from well-fed eyes. Jealous, He snarled. SHE arched, threw Him already chewed food and left. *He'll be back, come fall, with something different on his mind,* and with that SHE scurried up the hillside and disappeared into the trees.

He sniffed the food. He had had experience with eating too quickly in a starving state. He pecked at the mash, swallowed patiently, let it settle, then pecked a little more. Hours passed before he finished. He could feel the old strength coming back. It filled Him with the confidence of the capable and well-fed. His mind did not function well yet, so he forgot where the mash had come from. By morning, he rose strong and agile.

Sound. The wondrous sound of life touched his ears. Birdsong, muskrat, rabbit, even the dull hum of moles burrowing beneath the land made Him dizzy with happy anticipation. No memories of a treasured life, rich with children, intruded upon his glee at the paradise of living meat He had been cast into.

He could not be blamed for not knowing this mountain was special, a place apart from the rest of the world, rich with plant life that was endlessly available. *The bird in front of me will do,* and he stalked it, though it wasn't really necessary in this place. No animals had any idea other animals would eat them. Bird pecked at the seeds about him, leaving the leaves for Him, and nodded in innocent greeting. He looked a little strange to bird, prancing about like that, but bird carried on eating nonchalantly.

Crunch, her neck broke, blood spilled, a scream from her throat issued forth and it was all over. Several of her family rushed to the scene. He went wild. Eyes bulging with the memory of hunger, he exacted bloody carnage on them all. Screams of perishing birds filled the air. Others came, batting wing against flesh, pecking at Him until, exhausted, he fell to the ground. Bones of bird lay scattered in great numbers. The living relatives of those who owned the bones stared in silence.

After a time, they spoke. "He looks like SHE, but there is something different about Him." ... "Where did he come from?" ... "The water must have brought Him... hmnmn," and a profound respect and a wee bit of terror of the seas was born among them. Anger, new and uncontrolled, consumed the youth. "We should kill Him," they whispered to one another. "Why?" queried the old birds, "perhaps he is ill." "Vengeance," came the reply. Youth harangued at length, full of the sort of outrage peculiar to the young, righteous and lacking in foresight. The elder birds, fearful of the consequences of killing another person, counselled the young:

"We'll go see SHE first. He is, after all, one of hers." The young birds, angry as they were, lacked the courage to move without the sanction of their elders. (It was a different time.) Reluctantly, they agreed.

As with some gentle-hearted women who love too much, SHE excused Him. "He was not from here, he didn't under-stand our ways, he had been starved, something no one on this island mountain could possibly understand. Let us give Him a chance to grow accustomed to our ways and see." Time passed and he continued to eat small animals, despite the gentle admonitions of SHE. The birds grew passive about his habits as he had come to prefer the four-legged people to their own race. He had never repeated the carnage on them since his first day on the island and the bird world began to forget that once they had all considered themselves one people. The land abounded with little animal life and he seemed always well satisfied without threatening the survival of any single species. An old inertia settled in around the eating habits of Him, even among the animals.

SHE, try as she might, could not convince Him to eat the plant mash everyone else ate. That it was better food seemed irrelevant to Him. As sometimes happens among people, certain curious individuals attracted by someone else's bizarre behaviour are influenced to emulate that behaviour. So it was that rat was the first to note that meat filled the body with a pleasant kind of fullness which was good for dreaming. A lazy relaxation resulted from the consumption of flesh and seemed better than the fulfilling quick energy of the mash.

Despite his eating habits, SHE loved Him and was soon pregnant. Her knowledge of birth, creation, was scanty. The change in her body was marvelous. The children came in great numbers, soft and sweet, full of innocent trust and com-plete dependence upon her. SHE thought, as some women are wont to think, that children would bring love to the tortured soul of her mate. SHE awaited his transformation.

It didn't come. His soul had perished in the sea of forgotten dreams. One morning SHE awoke with one less child. Rage, Shock, Grief, all made her crazy for a moment; then practical necessity cooled her emotions and SHE packed up her remaining children and retreated to a secret lair in which to nurture them. His blood and his cynicism filled the souls of some of them, while the others tended to be like her. Hunting tiny prey came naturally to those like Him, and they set about capturing and consuming mice against her wishes. SHE, loving mother that she was, remained forever disappointed at their misbehaviour, but could not bring herself to disdain her young. SHE nourished them in the way they chose.

Her eldest son had a penchant for birds, and like his father, felt territorial mastery deep in his loins. He forbade birds in his kingdom, eating them should they transgress onto his territory. The old rage came back to the birds whose land base and freedom shrank under the dominion of this prodigal.

In the night, second son dreamed of his sister, tender and warm, and he sought her. At first she resisted, but eventually her time came and she succumbed to the perpetuation of her species. The cynicism of their father was assured in their union. Like a prairie fire, the heady, dream-like satisfaction which followed the consumption of meat spread. Muskrat ate fish, fox ate rabbit, rat ate mouse and deep sadness settled in SHE. Her union with Him had brought pain to the land and it grew too large for SHE to bear. As SHE lay in her cavern, nursing a new batch of children to independence, SHE let go one last whimper and died.

*   *   *

Old eagle watched this and wondered at the meaning of all this change. She watched somewhat dispassionately, thinking SHE had always been too soft-hearted, but SHE's mate was swinging the world too much in the other direction. Eagle felt SHE loved too much, too earnestly, and in the end, was consumed by it. A cold shiver travelled up old eagle's

spine as she realized that perfection had died as a human quality with the passing of SHE.

The bird people learned to fly away whenever the citizens
of the four-legged race approached them. A youthful eagle,
sharp-eyed and brilliant (in a military sort of way), noted the
bird people outnumbered the four-legged people. He counselled the others to war. "The largest among us can deplete
the smallest and most numerous of them. Hawk, take mole,
mouse and the children of muskrat. I shall have raccoon, rabbit and the children of cougar and fox; gull take fish; you small
birds can take worm, insect and spider. Together, we can rule
the land. Terror will drive the animal race back into the sea."

Now this was curious. Eagle wondered at such folly.
Since when has command of the plant world ever been a goal
for either race of people? Still, eagle said nothing. And it
came to pass, the four-legged and the winged people went to
war. (Now modern men of the two-legged variety, who say
they alone are people, claim they invented war and refer to
1914-1918 as the First World War, but eagle and raven know
differently. Unlike two-legged men, the winged and the four-
legged people gave it up the first time.)

Bat is a strange bird-animal. His disposition is different
from any other person's. He sometimes walks on two legs and
flies at other times. It matters little what he eats so long as he
does. He eats without conscience. His one great love is himself. He watched the conflict between the people heat up. Interesting. He was sure it had nothing to do with him. The
birds converged in their great numbers upon the animals, consuming their flesh and letting much blood flow. Bat flew about
cheering them on, sometimes partaking in the carnage. The
animals' wits sharpened by the attack, they stalked bird nests
and slew the young. Bat joined them too, walking about,
stalking bird nests and laying to rest their young.

An odd joy filled the bat. He was proud of his ability to
walk and fly with equal comfort. The war intensified, each
side polarizing, growing experienced, becoming more and

more sophisticated in the business of war. No one called it art then, as some men do today. Carnage, strategizing and greater carnage abounded. Blood filled the mountain, covered the earth, and the smell of death filled the air. Animals learned to climb trees and destroy nests; birds ferreted out the newborn animals whose parents had gone to the water's edge to quiet their thirst. And bat, unnoticed, joined whichever side was winning the war.

Old eagle watched the war, wept with pity at the antics of bat, and was bothered by the scent of death which contaminated their home, but she was not so faint of heart to be saddened beyond living, as SHE had been. Eagle had not experienced love of mate in the same way. *No mate should ever pull the character from out of your soul—love or no love.* Eagle remembered her old mate and chuckled at the memory. She saw him tucking his old white head beneath his wing and worrying the down underneath it. She had had, at the time of his death, a funny desire to go first. Now she thought it was just as well it had gone the other way; the ridiculous picture of their grandchildren participating in the death below would have been too much for the old man. (In those days gentleness was not a trait of only one sex.)

Raven perched herself just below eagle. *How does Raven always know when I am lost in deep thought?* old eagle wondered, but didn't say. She whistled out a bored "Hello and how are you?" Raven's voice annoyed eagle, but she had the redeeming quality of subverting the annoying stridence of her voice by always coming to the point and talking little. Eagle liked that. "We have to stop the war." Eagle knew Raven meant she should think of something Raven could do to stop it. "What we need is a screaming wind, a tornado, to bring them to hysteria. We need to have wind sing a lamenting song of their lost ones. We need them to hear their lost ones wail sobs of recrimination at their grandchildren," eagle said. "That will mean the old ones will have to do all the work of bringing conscience to their grandchildren, perhaps just a windsong to counsel them to meet and do the right thing. You could speak, eagle, and I will bring the wind and gather them together," was Raven's response. "Sounds all right to me," eagle said, shrugging diplomatically. Raven drew the wind and the voices of the lost ones to the ears of the living.

Under the hysteria of the wind and the song of their ancients, the carnage stopped. Animal and bird people gathered, each forming a half circle that met the half circle of the other. The smallness of the numbers in the circle stunned them; the magnitude of death caused by war shamed them.

Now eagle is no idealist. Practical reality had changed them; she knew they could not return to the old ways. The mash had been destroyed by fire sparked by the burn-and-destroy policy of the people at one stage of the war; neither could they negate the new feeling of territory which now filled each animal and bird. What they could do was come to an agreement on the law of survival which would govern the people.

Eagle recounted the history of the war, how it came to be, the numbers of dead, and determined the course to be taken should they all agree. She calculated how much meat each animal, bird and bat would need to guarantee survival. They listened. She spoke of survival of the plant world, who should eat plants, who should eat meat and how many births each race should have so no population should over-run the others. She postulated that birds should have dominion over the skies and animals dominion over the land, but neither should rule the place of their dominion. Should birds need rest, trees should provide them with a home. Large animals should not rob nests. Each animal and bird was given a prey, food which would challenge their strength and yet assure their survival. No one would have any more than the bare necessities. Eagle restricted her own movement to gliding on the wind currents, and all were well-satisfied, except Raven. Raven was sure all things were not taken care of. There was bat, so confused about his identity and the nature of the gathering that he strutted about and flew by turns. Raven leapt into the air, wings beating furiously, and plucked the vision from bat's eyes. Eagle banished bat to fly only at night, never to be part of either race of people. A general commotion arose, but in the end bird and animal people all agreed to ostracize bat, but in order to protect against arbitrary judgement the people exacted a promise from eagle and Raven that no ostracism should ever take place again without the consent of all the people. Raven and eagle agreed.

Content, eagle continued to live for some time after. She watched the water recede as the earth shed less tears for her children. Quietly, death came. It filled her bones with the need to rest for all eternity and bestirred memories of her mate worrying his wing. She smiled a soft grin of one musing over old familiar things and fell from her perch.

Press Gang Publishers Feminist Co-operative is committed to
publishing a wide range of writing by women which explores themes
of personal and political struggles for equality.

A free listing of our books is available from Press Gang Publishers,
603 Powell Street, Vancouver, B.C. V6A 1H2 Canada